A New Library of
the Supernatural

Magic, Words, and Numbers

Magic,

Words, and Numbers

by Stuart Holroyd

Doubleday and Company, Inc. Garden City, New York, 1976

Series Coordinator: John Mason
Design Director: Günter Radtke
Picture Editor: Peter Cook
Editor: Sally Burningham
Copy Editor: Mitzi Bales
Research: Sarah Waters
General Consultant: Beppie Harrison

Library of Congress Cataloging in Publication Data

Holroyd, Stuart
Magic, Words, and Numbers
(A New Library of the Supernatural; v. 7)
1. Magic 2. Cabala I. Title II. Series
BF1611.H64 133 75-26142
ISBN 0-385-11313-7

Doubleday and Company
ISBN: 0-385-11313-7

Library of Congress Catalog
Card No. 75-26142

A New Library of the Supernatural
ISBN: 11327-7

© 1975 Aldus Books Limited, London

Printed and bound in Italy by
Amilcare Pizzi S.p.A.
Cinisello Balsamo (Milano)

**Frontispiece: a witch in danger from invoked demons.
Above: Roman magical hand to avert the evil eye.**

EDITORIAL CONSULTANTS:

COLIN WILSON
DR. CHRISTOPHER EVANS

Most of us would like to have power—power to gain what we wish, power to do what we want, even power over others. For centuries men and women have sought such power in the rituals and formulas of magic. Some have turned to the ancient wisdom of the Cabala; some have looked for hidden significance in words; others have believed that numbers hold the key. But all of them have tried to understand and influence the mysterious world in which we all live. Their search is a fascinating one, and records—often fragmentary—still exist that hint at what they discovered and what powers they succeeded in controlling. However, the tantalizing question remains: Are there laws, other than the familiar laws of Nature, that people can use to gain special and remarkable powers?

1

Chance, Magic, and Synchronicity

Some years ago George D. Bryson, an American businessman, was making a trip from St. Louis to New York. He decided to break his journey in Louisville, Kentucky, a town he had never visited before. At the station he inquired for somewhere to stay, and was directed to the Brown Hotel. He went there, found they had a room—number 307—and registered. Then, just for a joke and because he had nothing better to do, he idly wandered over to the mail desk and asked if there was any mail for him. To his astonishment and consternation the receptionist calmly handed him a letter addressed to Mr. George D. Bryson, Room

There are jokes about the long arm of coincidence, but behind them lies the serious problem: what does coincidence mean? Is there significance which we have learned to ignore in many oddly related happenings, unexplained by our usual expectations in a world normally made meaningful by the laws of cause-and-effect? Above: a searcher shows how a dead man's hair looked when he was found in a treacherous swamp. Right: the next day, before he was notified of the accident, the dead man's brother painted this.

6

7

"A challenge to our assumptions about reality..."

Just before his brother's death —apparently of a heart attack while gathering water lilies in a swamp—German artist Gerfried Schellberger was obsessed by images of a man with his hair swept forward into a point, by images of death symbolized by a horse-drawn hearse, and by water lilies. The artist himself was troubled by his work, sensing uneasily that it had a meaning.

307. On investigation it turned out that the previous occupant of the room had been another George D. Bryson, who worked with a firm in Montreal.

We have all had similar strange experiences that we put down to coincidence, chance, or luck. Because these experiences are so common, scientists and philosophers have begun to wonder whether there is more to them than mere chance or coincidence. With this focusing of scientific and philosophical interest, more and more evidence has come to light that both the world we live in and the lives we lead are more mysterious than we usually suppose. In order to explain otherwise inexplicable events, many Westerners have taken a fresh look at magic and the psychic sciences.

Our normal way of looking at things in the West is from the standpoint of cause and effect. We have a built-in habit of mind that tries to make sense of events by seeing them as if they are linked in a chain, one leading to another. But, as the Scottish philosopher David Hume pointed out over two centuries ago, this is only a useful working method, not an absolute truth. When one billiard ball meets another and the second moves away, we cannot see cause and effect taking place. We can only assume that it does so. This kind of assumption is fairly safe as long as it is confined to practical observations, but unfortunately Western society has gone much further than that. It has raised the cause and effect link to the status of a general law, and in doing so has often tended to exclude other points of view. Events such as chance or coincidence, which cannot be explained by a logical cause and effect sequence, are all too easily dismissed by many people as incomprehensible.

Eastern philosophers did not fall into this pattern of thinking, and the growing attention being paid to Eastern philosophies in the West is both an indication of dissatisfaction with the mechanistic laws of cause and effect, and a realization that there are other ways of looking at life.

What we call coincidental or chance events are a challenge to our fundamental assumptions about reality. When many of them accumulate they build up a solid credibility barrier—like the sound barrier built up in front of an aircraft flying at supersonic speed. We then have to crash this barrier to break through. We have to acquire a new conception of a reality beyond the credibility barrier created by our expectations and assumptions, particularly the assumption of cause and effect. In 1973 a book called *The Challenge of Chance* was published in London. Written by Sir Alister Hardy, Robert Harvie, and Arthur Koestler, it contains many anecdotes illustrating apparent chance or coincidence. These examples may help us to look at things in a new way.

One is about a scholar who had been preparing some of his lectures for publication. He died suddenly, leaving a request for his son to see the work through. Checking the typescript and completing the footnotes took the son six months of devoted labor. Finally he was left with the last and most difficult query to solve. It was a reference from one of the 36 volumes of Sacred Books of the East. But which one? There was nothing to guide him. As a last resort he decided to take home three of the volumes

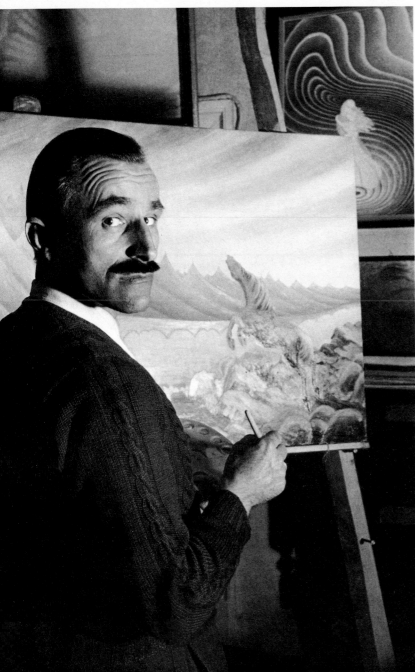

Above: Norbert Schellberger, the man who died in the swamp. He had just returned to his family at the end of World War II, and was visiting his parents with his wife and their child. His death was not only sensed by his artist brother, but also by both parents and an aunt. She had strange, distressing dreams about him just before he died so unexpectedly. Left: Gerfried Schellberger at his easel with one of the paintings. Below: Gerfried's painting of a bearded man with hair in a point, done just before Norbert's death.

that his father had once borrowed from the library. Sitting in his study late that evening, he uttered a sort of prayer to his father saying "Can't you be allowed to help me?" He picked up one of the volumes at random—and opened it at the very page he needed.

Another incident concerns a man who bought a house from two elderly ladies on the condition that a certain picture must never be removed from its position. It remained there until he sold the house several years later, when he sent the picture to a salesroom. The new owner of the house, who knew nothing about the picture, bought it and hung it back in the spot where it had always been.

9

Above: a man reported a vivid dream that woke him "in a cold sweat," in which his car ran over a small boy who darted in front of him. Below: weeks later, driving into Manchester, England, he saw a child dash out. He swerved violently, missing him by inches. He leaped out of the car—and was staggered to recognize the child of his dream.

The following story won a contest sponsored by an English newspaper to find the best example of chance. George Feifer, an American author living in London, lent a friend an advance copy of his new novel *The Girl From Petrovka*. It was covered with red marks because Feifer had been correcting it for the American edition. A week later the friend reported that he had lost the copy from his car. The author was understandably and exceedingly annoyed because he had to make the corrections all over again.

Two years later when Feifer was in Vienna for the filming of his novel, one of the actors told him about a strange incident. After the actor had heard that he would be in the film of *The Girl From Petrovka*, he tried one day to buy a copy of the book in order to familiarize himself with the character and plot. He was unsuccessful. While waiting for his train in the London subway, however, he noticed a book lying on a bench. On picking it up he saw to his astonishment that it was *The Girl From Petrovka*, the very book he had searched for in vain all afternoon. He was puzzled by the many red marks in it and showed it to Feifer. The surprised author instantly recognized it as the copy that had been lost two years before.

To shrug off events like these as "just chance" may be to shut off a significant area of knowledge. The eminent psychologist C. G. Jung certainly thought they were worth serious investigation. Over the years he noticed that both he himself and his patients had had many experiences of what he called "meaningful coincidences." Many of these involved dreams or premonitions, and he devoted much time toward the end of his life in attempting to explain these experiences. Jung used the term *synchronicity* to describe incidents that seemed to be connected by time and meaning, but not by cause and effect. He felt that these coincidences, in some way, had their roots in very strong unconscious feelings that at certain times of stress or change came to the surface. He gives several examples of this happening in his own life.

One day, as he was returning home by train, he was overpowered by the image of someone drowning. He was so upset that he was unable to read, and could only wonder whether there had been some sort of accident. When he got home he was met by his grandchildren, and discovered from them that the youngest had fallen in the lake and had almost been drowned. The little boy had been fished out just in time by his older brother. This nearly fatal accident had happened at exactly the time that the idea of someone drowning had occurred to Jung.

Many of us have had odd dreams and premonitions about our family or friends that have turned out to be true. As a psychoanalyst Jung also had a very close relationship with his patients. One night when Jung was sleeping alone in a hotel after a lecture, he awoke with a start. He was convinced that someone had opened the door and entered the room, but when he switched on the light, there was no one to be seen. He then tried to remember what had happened. He had been wakened by a feeling of dull pain as if something had struck his forehead and the back of his skull. The following day he received a telegram informing him that a former patient, whom he had lost touch

The Train That Stopped

It was November 1971 in London on a day like any other. In one of the city's subway stations, a train was approaching the platform. Suddenly a young man hurled himself directly into the path of the moving train. The horrified driver slammed on the brakes, certain that there was no way to stop the train before the man was crushed under the wheels. But miraculously the train did stop. The first carriage had to be jacked up to remove the badly injured man, but the wheels had not passed over him and he survived.

The young man turned out to be a gifted architect who was recovering from a nervous breakdown. His amazing rescue from death was based on coincidence. For the investigation of the accident revealed that the train had not stopped because of the driver's hasty braking. Seconds before, acting on an impulse and completely unaware of the man about to throw himself on the tracks, a passenger had pulled down the emergency handle, which automatically applies the brakes of the train. The passenger had no particular reason for doing so. In fact, the Transport Authority considered prosecuting him on the grounds that he had had no reasonable cause for using the emergency system!

with after helping through a severe crisis, had shot himself. The bullet had lodged at the back wall of the skull.

Synchronistic events of this kind frequently happened to Jung and his patients. He became convinced that they had a deep significance, and he applied his tremendous knowledge, experience, and diligence to the task of discovering their meaning. When he died he was working on the idea that physics and psychology would ultimately come together under a common concept that would be a unifying key to the forces at work in the physical and psychical worlds. Physicists had released the energy locked away in the atom. Might it not be possible, he wondered, to likewise release the energy locked away in the human psyche? Throughout the ages magicians have aspired to just such a unity of the physical and psychical worlds, though they do not work in a scientific way.

One of the world's oldest books is the ancient Chinese book of wisdom and divination, the *I Ching* or Book of Change. The source of the *I Ching* is shrouded in myth, but it was systematized in its present form by King Wen in 1143 B.C., and later clarified by his son the Duke of Chou. This famous book has exerted enormous influence on the two main Chinese religions, Confucianism and Taoism. It is still widely revered and consulted in the Far East today. Since the first translation into English in 1882, the *I Ching* has gained many Western followers. One of these was Jung, who devoted a great deal of time and thought to its study.

The *I Ching* is based on a belief in the unity of man and the surrounding universe. The universe is thought to be made up of two equal and complementary forces, Yang and Yin. Yang is the active principle and stands for positive qualities. Yin, passive but equally important, stands for the negative. Yang stands for light and Yin for dark. Since everything is made up from Yang and Yin, differences between things are due to different proportions of Yang and Yin. According to ancient Chinese belief, every event results from an interaction between these two principles.

The *I Ching* contains 64 figurations, each a different combination of six broken and unbroken lines and therefore called a hexagram. The broken lines represent Yin, and the unbroken lines Yang. Each hexagram has a symbolic name signifying a different condition of life, and is accompanied by a short explanatory text attributed to King Wen. There is also a commentary on the text, possibly by Confucius, as well as explanations of the symbolism of the hexagram and the meaning of the separate lines in each hexagram. The *I Ching* does not regard the future as fixed. It does not aim to tell those who consult it what will happen, but tries to give guidance at the highest moral level so that an individual can determine what the correct course of action would be. Because this guidance depends to a large degree on perceptive interpretation, it is vital that the questioner approach the book in a serious frame of mind.

The *I Ching* is a system of wisdom containing advice, moral precepts, and insights that may guide the questioner. In order to find out which particular hexagram is relevant to his or her particular situation, the questioner tosses three coins six times.

Below: Carl Gustav Jung, the world-famous Swiss psychiatrist who died in 1961. He worked for a time with Freud, but parted company with him and went on to develop his own theories of the unconscious and the importance it has in human life. For Jung, a most important problem was how the conscious mind communicated with the extended and enriched world of the unconscious so that it could play a full part in the life of the individual.

Above: Chinese priests in a
temple tossing bamboo tallies
to determine the success of
their prayers. The picture is
by an English artist, William
Alexander, who accompanied Lord
Macartney's embassy to China
in 1792. Alexander kept a very
detailed record of what he saw.
Left: a red lacquer panel with
pa kua, the eight *I Ching* trigrams
made up of broken and unbroken
lines. Two trigrams together create
a hexagram of the ancient book.
The trigrams encircle the inter-
locked yin and yang symbols, seen
as the opposing but complementary principles of the universe.

Above: a Taoist priest's robe embroidered with the *pa kua* trigrams. In the center are the all-important symbols of yin and yang. The origins of the *I Ching* are veiled in tradition and myth, but its elements are more than 4000 years old and so predate both Taoism and Confucianism.

(Fifty yarrow stalks may also be used but coins are more common today). Each toss will indicate a line in the hexagram, working up from the bottom line. For example, if the first throw of the coins shows two tails and one head, the bottom line would be an unbroken one. The hexagram formed in this way by the six tosses is the one to be consulted and interpreted.

The American psychologist Ira Progoff recalls an occasion when he consulted the *I Ching* with Jung's help. He had published a first book on Jung's work and had come to Europe from America to continue his research under the great man's guidance. One afternoon when they were sitting in the garden of Jung's house beside Lake Zurich Jung asked him if he had ever used the *I Ching*. When Progoff said he had not, Jung suggested they do so there and then, and asked him what problem he would like to put to the *I Ching*. Progoff said he had no particular problem at that time, but he had general questions about his present situation and the meaning and eventual outcome of what he was doing. Jung produced three coins from an old worn leather purse. On tossing the coins six times, Progoff was directed to hexagram 59, named "dispersion." Hexagram 59 looks like this:

The text is as follows:

Dispersion. Success. The king approaches his temple. It furthers one to cross the great waters. Perseverence furthers.

This seemed relevant to Progoff's situation. He had just published a book that aimed to spread or disperse Jung's ideas, so he was encouraged by the indication that it would be a success. He had crossed "the great waters" of the Atlantic to come and work with Jung. He was enjoying a period of great good fortune in an idyllic situation (the "temple" in the second line symbolizes a place of safety). Finally, his chief worry was that in the circumstances he might be taking his life and work too easily, so the words "perseverence furthers" were particularly meaningful to him.

It was all relevant enough. But why, Progoff asked, should the act of throwing some coins in a garden in Switzerland in 1953 get a reading from an ancient Chinese text that had a specific personal meaning for him? It seemed impossible and absurd. Or was it just chance? Superficially it looked like chance, but a highly sophisticated civilization had made practical use of the book and of the principle underlying it over a period spanning many centuries. That was a fact that could not be lightly dismissed. A man like Jung had certainly not dismissed it.

In *Memories, Dreams and Reflections* Jung describes his long-standing fascination with the *I Ching*. He had begun experimenting with it in about 1920, and one summer he decided to launch an all-out attempt to solve the riddle of the book. Instead of the traditional yarrow stalks, he cut himself a bunch of reeds.

He wrote: "I would sit for hours beneath the 100-year-old pear tree, the *I Ching* beside me, practicing the technique . . . in an interplay of questions and answers. All sorts of undeniably remarkable results emerged—meaningful connections with my own thought processes which I could not explain to myself." Jung was preoccupied with the question of whether or not the *I Ching's* answers were significant. If they were significant, how did this connection between the psychic and the physical come about? How could a problem in the mind of a questioner be answered by the interpretation of an ancient hexagram, seemingly selected at random?

Later he tried using the *I Ching* with his patients and found that a fairly high proportion of answers seemed to be appropriate. He describes one case involving a young man with a strong mother complex. He wanted to get married, and had found a girl who seemed suitable. However, he was uneasy, fearing that unconsciously he may have been attracted by another strong mother figure. He consulted the *I Ching,* and the text of his hexagram seemed appropriate to his predicament. It read "The maiden is all powerful. One should not marry such a maiden."

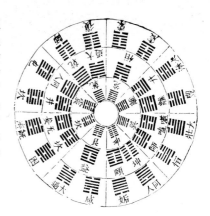

Above: the hexagrams of the *I Ching* taken from a 16th-century Chinese encyclopedia of wisdom. Below: consulting the oracle. Steady concentration is required to calculate the lines properly. It is also necessary to keep the question clearly in the mind.

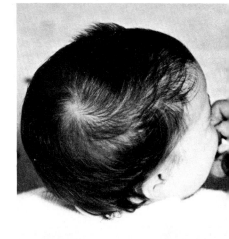

One of the most fascinating of Nature's corresponding patterns is the spiral. It appears all around us. Our galaxy, like the galaxies around us, whirls into infinite space in the shape of a spiral; water spirals downward and to the right in a whirlpool; the hair on our heads grows in a spiral around the crown; and the head of a daisy is a double spiral as well. The foundation of all life, the DNA molecule that carries the genetic message for each living cell, is organized in a deceptively simple double spiral in which to lock its code.

Jung's suggestion of how the *I Ching* works was the same as his theory on meaningful chance. This, as we have seen, was that events can be linked to each other by time and meaning, although they are in no way associated by cause and effect. In the idea of cause and effect, events evolve out of one another. In the idea of meaningful chance or synchronicity, objective events are in some way interdependent, as though bound together by a vast network of relationships. This network in turn is linked up with the psychic or subjective state of the person involved. In the case of the *I Ching* this person would be the questioner.

A belief in the interaction between man and the universe, or mind and matter, is fundamental to the theory and practice of magic the world over. Equally fundamental is the idea that there are favorable conditions for such interactions, conditions that involve the shapes, the patterns, and even the relationships in space between the elements in a given situation. These condi-

tions do not appear to depend on any direct cause and effect relationship or, at any rate, any relationship that we at the moment can understand. For example, there seem to be favored positions for the siting of holy places. Propitious times for certain actions appear to depend on the positions of the planets. Certain shapes are said to afford protection, bring good fortune, or attract evil powers. Are all such beliefs merely superstitions? Anyone inclined to dismiss them as such without further thought might also consider that many strange facts have been demonstrated in recent years, for which there seem as yet to be no known explanation. Blunt razor blades become sharp again if left inside a miniature model pyramid. Wounded mice heal more quickly if they are put in spherical cages. Shape, it appears, exerts some influence that we cannot explain.

Supposing we are prepared to recognize the limitations of looking at everything from the viewpoint of cause and effect, where does it get us? Perhaps not far, but it leaves us free to follow up clues and play with possibilities. Take, for example, the idea of shapes and patterns. We find that Nature, in fact, has only a small repertoire of basic shapes and patterns, and that the same ones tend to crop up in widely different contexts. A tungsten atom magnified two million times looks like a constellation of stars in the sky. When the 18th-century physicist Ernst F. Chladni found a way of making sound waves visible by mounting a metal plate covered with sand on a violin and drawing a bow across the strings, the sand arranged itself in patterns commonly found in living organisms. There is an intricate network of pattern and structure correspondences throughout the universe, and these patterns do not seem to have any causal connection.

Could events be thought of in the same way? Could a tiny change in the pattern of events existing at a given moment in time—a thing so small as a man throwing coins and formulating a question—affect the total existing situation and form a new pattern? Could this new pattern have the power to draw into relation to itself other events and situations remote in time and space? These were the kind of questions that Jung was asking. He even coined the term "magic causality" to describe such possibilities, which must have raised some eyebrows among his professional and academic colleagues. Here is an example of magic causality:

Henry, a patient undergoing analysis, had a dream in which his fate was decided by four Chinese who consulted an oracle "using little ivory sticks." His analyst drew his attention to the *I Ching*, and suggested that he should consult the book himself. Henry was 25 years old, highly intellectual, repressed, imaginative, and introverted. The hexagram he obtained when he consulted the book was the one called "youthful folly." Part of the commentary read: "For youthful folly, it is the most hopeless thing to entangle itself in empty imaginings. The more obstinately it clings to such unreal fantasies the more certainly will humiliation overtake it." Henry was shaken by the relevance of the reading. Till then he had denied the existence of anything except the purely rational. He had suppressed any feelings or thoughts that did not appear to be logical.

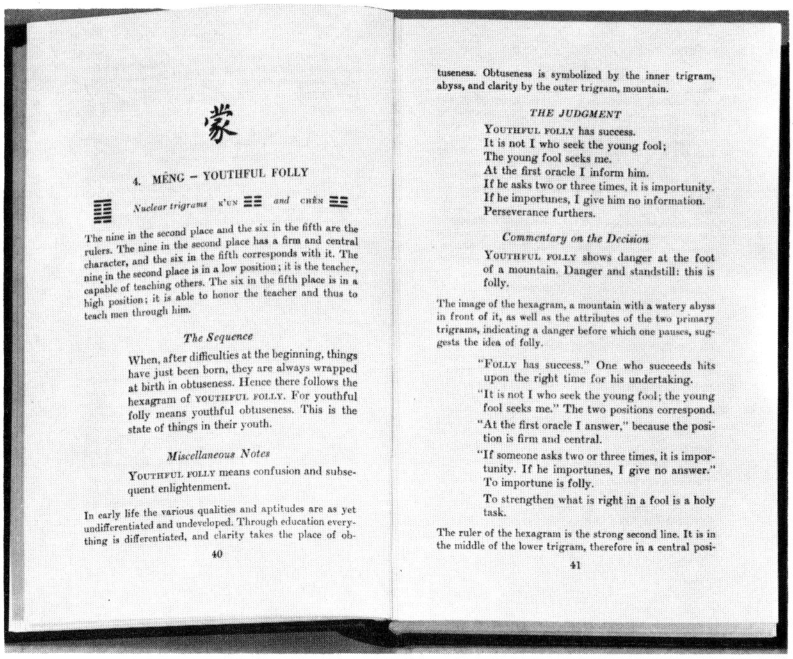

蒙

4. MÊNG – YOUTHFUL FOLLY

Nuclear trigrams K'UN ☷ *and* CHÊN ☳

The nine in the second place and the six in the fifth are the rulers. The nine in the second place has a firm and central character, and the six in the fifth corresponds with it. The nine in the second place is in a low position; it is the teacher, capable of teaching others. The six in the fifth place is in a high position; it is able to honor the teacher and thus to teach men through him.

The Sequence

When, after difficulties at the beginning, things have just been born, they are always wrapped at birth in obtuseness. Hence there follows the hexagram of YOUTHFUL FOLLY. For youthful folly means youthful obtuseness. This is the state of things in their youth.

Miscellaneous Notes

YOUTHFUL FOLLY means confusion and subsequent enlightenment.

In early life the various qualities and aptitudes are as yet undifferentiated and undeveloped. Through education everything is differentiated, and clarity takes the place of ob-

40

tuseness. Obtuseness is symbolized by the inner trigram, abyss, and clarity by the outer trigram, mountain.

THE JUDGMENT

YOUTHFUL FOLLY has success.
It is not I who seek the young fool;
The young fool seeks me.
At the first oracle I inform him.
If he asks two or three times, it is importunity.
If he importunes, I give him no information.
Perseverance furthers.

Commentary on the Decision

YOUTHFUL FOLLY shows danger at the foot of a mountain. Danger and standstill: this is folly.

The image of the hexagram, a mountain with a watery abyss in front of it, as well as the attributes of the two primary trigrams, indicating a danger before which one pauses, suggests the idea of folly.

"FOLLY has success." One who succeeds hits upon the right time for his undertaking.

"It is not I who seek the young fool; the young fool seeks me." The two positions correspond.

"At the first oracle I answer," because the position is firm and central.

"If someone asks two or three times, it is importunity. If he importunes, I give no answer." To importune is folly.

To strengthen what is right in a fool is a holy task.

The ruler of the hexagram is the strong second line. It is in the middle of the lower trigram, therefore in a central posi-

41

Left: Henry, a patient undergoing Jungian analysis, was referred to the *I Ching* by his therapist. This copy of the book is turned to the hexagram *Meng* or Youthful Folly, to which he was directed. He found it most relevant to his situation. However, in this hexagram he was warned against consulting the *I Ching* again—"If someone asks two or three times, it is importunity. If he importunes, I give no answer."

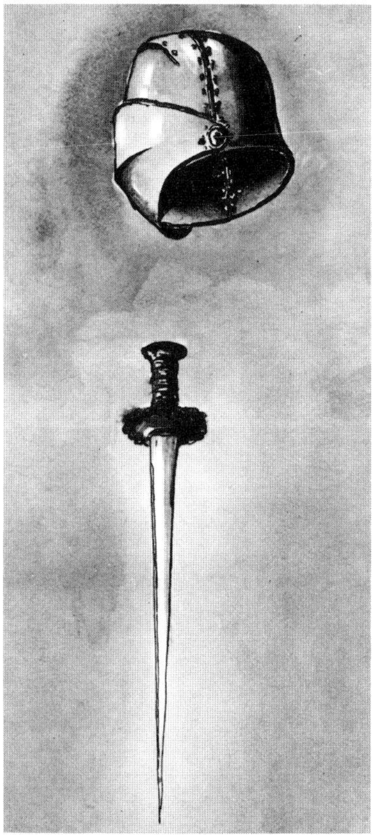

Above: Henry's drawing of the sword and helmet he saw in a dream. This dream led him to the *I Ching* again, and to a clearer appreciation of the part his unconscious played in his life.

The *I Ching* had told Henry not to consult the book again. However, one night he had a vivid dream of a helmet with a sword floating in empty space. On an impulse he opened the *I Ching* at random. The first words he read were: "The clinging is fire, it means coats of mail, helmets, it means lances and weapons." He was amazed. He suddenly understood that the reason he had been forbidden to consult the book again was to give his unconscious an opportunity to express itself unhampered by his rational mind. After this experience, his analyst reports, Henry "listened eagerly to the communications of his unconscious" and gradually became a changed man, "full of enterprising spirit."

Does magic involve the focusing of powers of the mind or the annexing of powers at work in the universe? This is a reasonable question. But it is wrongly phrased. The deeper we go into the matter the more clearly we realize that it is not a question of either/or but of both/and. Henry's case illustrates this. The images of a helmet and a weapon were *both* in his dream *and* in the external world as words printed in the book. A classic synchronistic event brought them together.

A fundamental principle of Jung's psychology is demonstrated in this. According to Jung the deepest structure of the human mind is the collective unconscious. This is made up from archetypes, which are not derived from personal experience but are in some way inherited. Archetypes in the Jungian use of the word are the distilled memories of the human species, and come from the common experience of mankind. They cannot be represented in verbal terms, but only by elusive symbols which, elusive as they are, we find are shared by all mythologies. They also provide patterns of behavior for all human beings in archetypal or stressful situations such as danger, conflict, death, or love. In such situations the archetypes, carrying strong emotions, invade the consciousness in the form of symbols.

According to Jung, it is by recognizing and coming to terms with the archetypal patterns in one's unconscious life that a person achieves wholeness, self-realization, and self-fulfillment. It was only when Henry listened to the communications of his unconscious that he was able to progress. It is at this unconscious level that humankind is in touch with the cosmic forces of Nature. It is by activating the archetypal symbol that a person acquires the extraordinary powers that are usually described as magical. Jung quotes the magician Albertus Magnus, who lived in the 13th century, as saying that everyone can influence everything magically if "he falls into a great excess." This corresponds with Jung's idea that by entering deeply into the unconscious we can activate the archetypes and achieve wholeness and power. It is like completing an electrical circuit. Until a contact is made nothing happens. But when it is made, power flows through the whole circuit. The contact on the psychic level is brought about when the individual's personal experience in depth corresponds with the universal archetype. This produces in the individual a sense of having an active and meaningful relationship to the whole, to life, and the world. This feeling is vital to psychological health.

Jung was interested in Albertus Magnus and in magic generally because he believed that the magician's power is of the same kind as that of the integrated individual, only greatly magnified. Magical power in his view is achieved by effecting a correspondence between the inner and outer, by completing a circuit that puts the individual into a dynamic relationship with the whole universe.

Bearing this in mind, let us take a closer look at the symbolic basis of the *I Ching*. As we have already seen, each of the 64 hexagrams consists of a different combination of unbroken and broken lines, the unbroken lines representing Yang, the active force in the universe, and the broken lines representing Yin, the equally important passive force. Each hexagram is made up of two trigrams, or groups of three lines. There are eight trigrams that are combined in 64 ways.

The trigrams are older than the *I Ching* itself. There is a tradition that they were first discovered by the Emperor Fu Hsi (2852–2738 B.C.), who saw them on the shell of a tortoise. In each trigram the lower line stands for earth, the middle line for man, and the top line for heaven. Thus man is seen as existing in a dynamic relationship of interaction between the heavens above and the earth below.

When three lines come together to form a trigram, there are eight possible combinations of broken and unbroken lines. Each trigram has an associated symbol, and these symbols form

Right: early in his analysis Henry recalled his earliest memory of getting a crescent roll from the baker's wife, and being proud that he was the only man present. Henry's drawing of the crescent is at the top of the picture. The crescent shape is still used on Swiss bakery shops, as in the photo in the middle. But the shape has long been linked with the moon and the feminine principle, as exemplified here by an image of the Babylonian goddess Ishtar, dating from the 3rd century B.C. She wears a crescent crown.

four groups of paired opposites: heaven and earth, mountain and lake, fire and water, thunder and wind. There are also associated pairs of qualities: the creative (heaven) and the receptive (earth), the violent (thunder) and the gentle (wind), the quiescent (mountain) and the joyous (lake), the clinging (fire) and the empty (water). When two trigrams come together to form a hexagram they will stand in varying degrees of accord or discord with each other. If they are in accord, the hexagram signifies something good, pleasant or fortunate. If they are in discord it signifies something bad, unpleasant, and unlucky. Take for example the following two hexagrams:

The one on the left is Peace, and the one on the right is Stagnation. In each hexagram Yin and Yang are in equal proportion, but are not intermixed. The hexagram on the left stands for harmony and balance because the three Yang lines of the lower trigram provide the strongest possible support for the three Yin lines in the upper one. But to have a Yang trigram bearing down with all its weight on a passive, yielding Yin trigram, as in the hexagram on the right, is most unfavorable.

In 1962 there was a tense international situation when massive Chinese forces gathered on the India-Tibet frontiers. The world expected them to swoop down on the plains of India. John Blofield, an Englishman then in Bangkok, consulted the *I Ching* for a prediction of what would happen. The oracle not only correctly foretold the Chinese strategy, but also gave reasons for it. This prediction was confirmed in newspaper reports after the event. Blofield, who later published his own translation of the *I Ching,* could not help wondering whether the Chinese generals had planned their campaign on the basis of the advice given by the venerable book. It was not improbable. In China's neighboring country of Japan, books of strategy based on the *I Ching* were required reading for military officers. Many Japanese believe that that fact accounted for the great victories they won in the early part of World War II, and one is reported to have said: "If the people at the very top had not been too 'modern' to consult the *Book of Change,* all those tremendous victories would not have been thrown away."

The significance of the hexagrams and their component trigrams is based on the assumption that all things in the universe, from solar systems to subatomic particles, are bound together in an intricate network of relationships, and are continually interacting with each other. Every part not only belongs to the whole, but also reflects the whole. The ancient Chinese considered the turtle sacred because its convex shell with its squares and lateral crossings corresponded exactly to the pattern of the heavens as they saw it. They would have agreed with the principle that is central to the magical system of the Hermetic philosophers.

Above: in Jung's ideas, his concept of archetypes—unconscious memories of the experiences of our ancestors which come into our consciousness as symbols during stress—plays a central role. Among the archetypes that appear in our dreams is that of the Self personified as a wise old man. This painting by Jung is a personification that appeared in one of his own dreams—a winged old man who carried keys. Jung said that this was a symbol representing superior insight.

Above: the personification of the Self is not always wise and old. Here, in a painting of one of his dreams by the artist Peter Birkhäuser, the Self is a marvelous youth, riding on a mysterious beast.

Left: another archetype is that of the fallen angel Lucifer, shown here as the resplendent bringer of light, but carrying the dual aspect of the Devil Satan. The idea of the basic duality of the universe runs through many of the philosophies that man has evolved to explain the cosmos and his own place in it.

23

Their principle is expressed in the simple formula "As above, so below," which has significance in mysticism as well as magic.

The Hermetic writings are a group of works on many subjects including the occult. The authors are unknown and the tracts probably span several centuries, the earliest dating back to the 3rd century B.C. The writings have been grouped under the name of Hermes Trismegistus, or thrice-greatest, the Greek name for the Egyptian god Thoth. Thoth was believed to be the scribe of the gods and the inventor of writing and all the arts dependent on it, including medicine, astronomy, and magic. The Greeks identified him with their own god, Hermes, the messenger of the gods, whose staff of entwined serpents symbolized wisdom. Hermes Trismegistus still remains an important figure in the occult tradition of the West.

One of the underlying hermetic beliefs was that the universe, or Cosmos, was a unity, and all its parts were interdependent. The relationship of all the parts was governed by the laws of sympathy and antipathy, but these could only be understood by divine revelation. The hermetic writings on alchemy included the system of occult sympathies, or correspondences, which underlies much magical tradition. This system aims to reveal secret links between various and apparently unconnected parts of the universe. Hermetic philosophy was of special interest to Jung, although he discovered it late in life—but not too late to devote ten years and two of his major works, *Psychology and Alchemy* and *Mysterium Coniunctionis*, to the study of it. This was a brave action at a time when alchemy was regarded as a discredited pseudoscience, and its devotees as absurdly misguided dabblers in chemistry or grasping charlatans. The professed aim of the alchemists—to change base metals into gold—seemed to personify human greed and credulity until Jung pointed out that the process was symbolical of man's attempt to change his own personality to attain a higher level of perfection. Jung discovered in the neglected hermetic literature a rich store of "archetypal motifs that . . . appear in the dreams of modern individuals." An archetype, remember, is an image or experience at a profound level, that enables the individual to come into contact with the universal and acquire extraordinary powers. Could the alchemists have found the secret of releasing the energy locked away in the human psyche, as the physicists later released the energy in the atom? Could they have succeeded in bringing together in dynamic interaction the physical and psychical worlds? Could they have been not misguided charlatans but profound philosophers and genuine magicians with powers over the material world?

The theory of synchronicity, Jung said, was an offshoot of his studies of the alchemists. It was a descriptive theory only, a statement that noncausal events are not mere accidents or chance but a significant part of reality that may provide the clue to some of the ultimate mysteries of life and the world. He stated that synchronistic events happened and were important, but he considered it beyond his mission as a scientist to say *how* they happened or whether they could be *made* to happen. Down the ages, however, there have been men less cautious about these questions—the magicians themselves.

Above: Jung, who took a fresh look at the tradition of alchemy and the whole symbolic system it incorporates, was fascinated with the work of Albertus Magnus, a well-known 13th-century magician. This illustration from the 1650 edition of Albertus Magnus' *Philosophia naturalis* shows man as the *anima mundi*, or world spirit, containing in his body the four elements of earth, water, fire, and air, and characterized by the number 10. This number represents perfection because it is the sum of 1 plus 2 plus 3 plus 4. These concepts play an important part in the alchemical tradition.

Right: a 16th-century manuscript illustration, rich in alchemical symbolism. It shows the rebirth of the soul in terms of medieval alchemy, which compares it to base metal that is transmuted into gold. The blackened soul emerging from the mire represents the first stage of transformation. The substance used to revive and whiten it is personified as the refined and all-powerful queen.

The Magical Correspondences

In 1934 the notorious gangster John Dillinger was gunned down by the FBI in Chicago. People rushed to the spot and mopped up the blood with handkerchiefs, bits of cloth or paper, hems of skirts and coats. It is said that afterward there was a brisk trade in the area in fake Dillinger blood—and some enterprising hustlers made another kind of "killing."

Long ago when a gladiator was killed in a Roman arena, epileptics rushed out to drink the fresh blood spurting from the wounds. In 1610 the dead bodies of over 50 peasant girls were found in the cellars of the Hungarian countess Elizabeth Bathory after she had

From the earliest beginnings, humans looked for meaning in the world around them, hoping if possible to control exterior events or at least to predict them. They deciphered patterns in the constellations moving overhead and eventually believed they had discovered the key to understanding celestial influences.

Right: the signs of the zodiac became correlated with the parts and functions of the human body, as shown in this zodiac figure from a 15th-century French manuscript.

Top: celestial influences could of course be unfavorable, and the prudent man created talismans to protect himself. This one was designed to give invisibility.

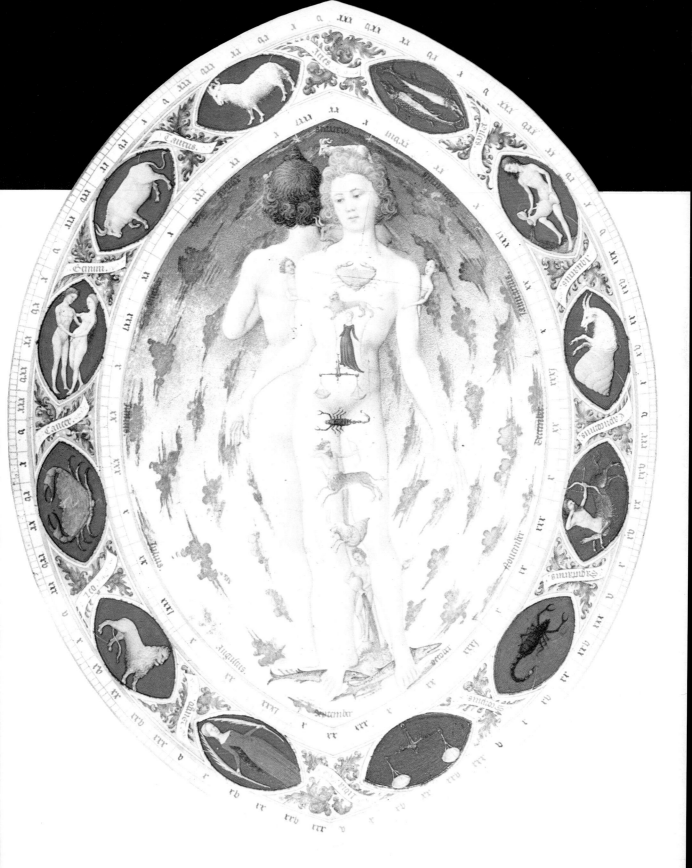

27

"The basis of all ritual magic"

been arrested. She had been in the habit of bathing in their blood in the hope that it would preserve her youthful looks.

Witches drank bats' blood believing that this would enable them to fly by night. Legends of vampires that suck human blood in order to sustain their vitality are worldwide, and so are black magic ceremonies involving bloody sacrifices. Belief in the magic properties of blood can be traced back to the fundamental principle of all magic: that the part reflects and contains the whole.

Aleister Crowley, a modern magician, took great care not to let his fingernail clippings or hair fall into anyone's hand in case a rival magician got hold of them and used them against him. What he had to fear is illustrated in the story of the Scottish schoolmaster who dabbled a bit in magic. He developed a passion for the elder sister of one of his pupils, and bribed the boy to bring him three of the girl's pubic hairs. While the boy was engaged in the delicate operation of obtaining the hairs from his sleeping sister, their mother caught him and made him tell her what he was doing. She sent the boy back to the schoolmaster with three hairs plucked from the udder of a heifer, and when the amateur magician worked his spell, he had an amorous heifer prancing around him and following him everywhere.

The crudest superstitions have in common with the subtlest arts of magic the belief that there exists a link between the part and the whole, and vice versa. This is a belief that is endorsed by great traditions of religious, philosophical, and scientific thought.

From earliest times magicians have been concerned with the influence of the sun, the moon, and the planets—all referred to as the planets for convenience—on human lives and events. They believed that there was a natural affinity between certain planets and certain colors, metals, animals, and plants. Magicians called these affinities *correspondences*. They were convinced that by understanding and using these correspondences correctly, they would be able to draw on the power of the planets. This system of correspondences is the basis of all ritual magic. Some of the main correspondences are shown in the table below.

Planet	Color	Metal	Stone	Creature
Saturn	black	lead	onyx	crocodile
Jupiter	blue	tin	sapphire	eagle
Mars	red	iron	ruby	horse
Sun	yellow	gold	topaz	lion
Venus	green	copper	emerald	dove
Mercury	gray	mercury	agate	swallow
Moon	white	silver	crystal	dog

Some of the correspondences seem fairly obvious, such as the association of the sun with the color yellow and the metal gold, and the moon with white and silver. Mercury, the fastest moving planet, is linked with the most mobile of metals of the same name, and with the fast-flying swallow. Saturn, the dimmest and

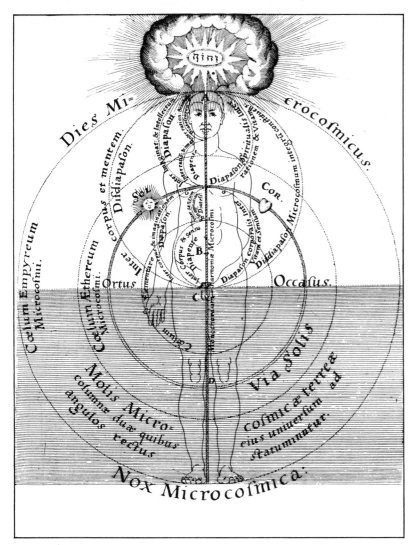

Left: Robert Fludd's concept of the correspondences between the universe—macrocosm—and man—microcosm. Like many other philosophers, Fludd envisioned the universe as a human organism on a gigantic scale. Fludd was an English physician active in the early 17th century. He became one of the leading members of the school of medical mystics who believed that their work was the key to universal science.

Below: the 15th-century Italian philosopher-doctor Marsilio Ficino based his belief in talismans on the idea that a charm made up of images and materials associated with a particular planet would hold within it the *spiritus* or essential substance of that planet. Magical correspondences would make it effective against unfavorable planetary aspects.

Below: pages from a 1548 German edition of *Naturalia* by Albertus Magnus. In it he links the magical and medicinal properties of herbs with planetary and zodiacal influences—the Martagon lily (left) with Saturn, and chicory (right) with the Sun, for example.

Below: Jupiter with its zodiac signs Pisces and Sagittarius, from a 15th-century Italian manuscript. Occupations thought in medieval times to be under Jupiter are shown at the bottom: an apothecary weighing out his materials, an alchemist sieving bags of sand to find precious metals, and a mathematician being consulted by a client. Each of the five then-known planets were given two zodiac signs, but the sun and moon had one each.

slowest moving planet, is associated with the color black and the heavy metal lead. Venus is the ruling power of nature as well as of love, and its association with nature's predominant color green follows logically. Since copper turns to green, it is the metal associated with Venus.

A magician who seeks to arouse and control the force of Venus, for example, would surround his working area with green draperies, and would wear a green robe possibly with a dove motif embroidered on it, a ring of emerald set in copper, and a Venus talisman. He would use a copper wand, or a wooden one capped with copper, and would burn the appropriate incense in a copper burner. He might also—though this is not essential—make a ritual sacrifice of a dove. He would

Below: a talisman of Jupiter. According to one authority, it must be made of tin with the image of an eagle's head in a six-pointed star on one side and a crown in a pentagram on the other. It can only be done on a Thursday. If all directions are carried out exactly, the talisman will protect the wearer against accident and certain diseases, as well as help to gain good-will and sympathy.

then be well disposed to draw down the cosmic influence of Venus, which may be employed to foster love or friendship, to secure pleasure, or to acquire beauty.

In 1489 Marsilio Ficino, a Florentine philosopher and physician, published a textbook of magical medicine, the *Libri de Vita* or Book of Life. It was based on a belief in sympathetic or natural magic, which used the system of correspondences. Powerful influences from the planets were said to be constantly pouring down on the earth. Colors or objects or plants especially associated with a particular planet would react to the planet and focus its influence.

Ficino suggests how men might use planetary influences to their best advantage. Young students are advised to avoid plants, herbs, stones, animals, and people that come under the influence of Saturn, because Saturn is the planet of melancholy influence and saps the forces of life and youth. Students should expose themselves to the more cheerful and life-giving influences of things associated with Jupiter, Venus, or the Sun. An illness is seen as often being the result of bad stellar influences, and a cure can be affected by drawing down from the heavens a stream of beneficial influences from the appropriate planet. To do this one must know which plants, stones, or metals belong to that planet, how to make the appropriate images, and at what astrological moment to do so. A substantial part of Ficino's book was devoted to instructions on making planetary images or talismans for medical use.

A talisman is an object that is worn or carried as a charm. It serves the purpose of either attracting or repelling various influences. To be effective, a planetary talisman should be made at a time when the relevant planet is pouring out its influences at maximum intensity, and should consist of an image engraved on the stone or metal associated with the planet. It should be made by the person who is going to wear it, who should cast his own horoscope to determine the hours most favorable for the work. The talisman should then be consecrated by being exposed to fumes produced by a prescribed mixture of herbs burned in an earthenware vessel over a fire made of certain types of wood. When this complex process has been completed the talisman should be worn on the breast in a silk pouch of a particular color.

Here is a brief description of the seven planetary talismans, their manufacture and use, and the powers traditionally ascribed to them:

1. The talisman of **Saturn** is engraved on a plaque of pure lead. On one side is an image of a bull's head enclosed in a six-pointed star, and on the other a scythe in a pentagram or five-pointed star. It must be made on a Saturday (Saturn's day), and consecrated over flames of alum, scammony, and sulphur burned on a fire of cypress and ash. It is worn in a blue silk pouch. It protects the wearer against death by apoplexy, cancer, consumption, or paralysis, against being buried alive while in a coma, and against assassination, poison, and ambush. It protects women in childbirth and is also useful in war because the enemy will not be able to cross any place that it is hidden.
2. The talisman of **Jupiter** is engraved on a plaque of pure tin.

The Consecration of a Talisman

In ritual magic the consecration of a talisman, or object worn as a charm, must be done in accordance with the law of correspondences which says that each planet is associated with a certain metal, color, animal, and plant. The illustration on the next page shows the consecration of a talisman for a person whose planet is Jupiter. It was one of the special and important ceremonies of the Order of the Golden Dawn.

The talisman had to be prepared in Jupiter's metal, which is tin, or color, which is violet, and was engraved with the symbols and numbers associated with Jupiter. Then, after performing banishing rituals to remove all outside influences, the members who had reached the grade that qualified them for performing the ceremony would chant invocations associated with Jupiter, and burn the particular incense of Jupiter. Next, with the most intense concentration and imagination, they used their psychic energies to summon down the energy from the sphere of Jupiter, drawing it down into the talisman. Finally, in a last banishing ritual, they would request "all spirits bound by this ceremony . . . to depart in peace unto their places." Only after all this, done exactly correct, was the talisman ready.

SATURN

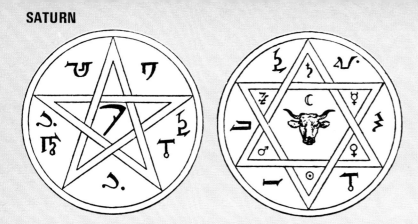

MARS

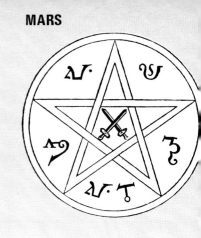

At about the same time that Ficino was working out his instructions for making talismans, the Swiss magician-physician Paracelsus was also studying the ancient works on talismans. Both he and Ficino were using authorities who took the doctrine from the secret traditions of Jewish mysticism, which were themselves believed to be derived from the occult sciences of Chaldea and Egypt. The talismans illustrated here are based on both Ficino's and Paracelsus' descriptions of effective planetary talismans.

It has on one side an image of an eagle's head in a six-pointed star, and on the other a crown in a pentagram. It must be made on a Thursday, and consecrated over fumes of frankincense, ambergris, balsam, cardomom, and saffron on a fire of oak, poplar, and fig. It is worn in a sky blue silk pouch. It protects the wearer against death by diseases of the liver or lungs or by unforeseen accidents, and it draws good-will and sympathy.

3. The talisman of **Mars** is engraved on a plaque of pure iron. On one side it has a lion's head in a six-pointed star and on the other two crossed swords in a pentagram. It must be made on a Tuesday, and consecrated over fumes of absinth and rue. It is worn in a red silk pouch. It protects the wearer against death by malignant ulcers or epidemic, and affords powerful protection against enemies. If concealed in a besieged citadel, it ensures that no attack from outside will suceed.

4. The talisman of the **Sun** is engraved on a plaque of pure gold and has a human head enclosed in a six-pointed star on one side, and a circle in a pentagram on the other. It must be made on a Sunday, and consecrated over fumes of cinnamon, saffron, and red sandalwood on a fire of laurel and dried heliotrope stalks. It is worn in a pouch of yellow silk. It protects the wearer against death by heart disease, epidemic, or conflagration, and draws the favor and good-will of people in high places.

5. The talisman of **Venus** is engraved on pure copper. On one side there is a dove in a six-pointed star, and on the other is the letter G in a pentagram. It must be made on a Friday, and

VENUS

MERCURY

consecrated over fumes of violets and roses on a fire of olive wood. It is worn in a green silk pouch. It protects the wearer against death by poisoning and, women in particular, against cancer. It preserves harmony in marriage, and if dipped in an enemy's drink, it will turn him into a friend for life.

6. The talisman of **Mercury** is engraved on a plaque made of an alloy of silver, tin, and mercury. It has a dog's head in a six-pointed star on one side, and a caduceus in a pentagram on the other. It must be made on a Wednesday, and consecrated over fumes of benzoin, mace, and storax on a fire of dried stalks of lilies, narcissus, and marjoram. It protects the wearer against attacks of epilepsy or madness, and against death by murder or poison. It is worn in a pouch of purple silk. If buried under a shop or place of business it insures prosperity, and if placed under the head during sleep, it brings prophetic dreams.

7. The talisman of the **Moon** is engraved on a plaque of pure silver and has on one side a goblet in a six-pointed star, and on the other a cresent in a pentagram. It must be made on a Monday, and consecrated over fumes of white sandalwood, camphor, aloes, amber, and cucumber seeds on a fire of dried stalks of artemisia, selenotrope, and ranunculus. It is worn in a white silk pouch. It protects the wearer against death by dropsy, apoplexy, madness, or shipwreck, and also protects people traveling in foreign lands.

The making of a personal planetary talisman involves detailed astrological calculations, and requires enormous patience and

MOON

Above: the making of a talisman from a Persian manuscript, dating from the early 16th century. The talisman in this case was believed to keep evil away from children. The painting shows pupils at a Koran school. They have a writing board with the word *nushreh*, which means talisman in Arabic, written on it. The text explains that this talisman is given to boys after they succeed in reading one of the 30 sections of the Koran.

dedication. It might work to a certain extent purely because of the faith invested in it. If it didn't work, the believer could always attribute the failure to some miscalculation, omission, or error in the complex process of making and consecrating it. However, we are not mainly concerned with the question of the effectiveness of talismans, but with the philosophy that lies behind them—the philosophy of a system of correspondences linking together nature, man, and the cosmos.

There is a story in Idries Shah's book *Oriental Magic* which shows that knowledge of a system of correspondences and belief in its power is worldwide. The story was related to the author by a Scotswoman who was married to an Afghan. She had an opportunity to witness and participate in the work of an Afghani alchemist, and she was convinced that he could actually make gold.

The process took days. On the first day the alchemist, Aquil Khan, led the woman and a friend miles into the jungle to find some plants like tall dandelions, from which they had to collect a thick white sap by breaking and squeezing the stalks. Throughout the long ritual Aquil Khan maintained complete silence and only communicated by signs. It was hours before he indicated that they had collected enough and could go home. On the second day at dawn they started out on another three-hour walk into the jungle, this time to collect some creamy yellow

mud from beside a stream. Out of this Aquil Khan made two deep bowls when they got back to his cave. On the third day they went out to collect special types of wood, and on the fourth to collect stones of a specific color, shape, and size. The fifth day they built a fire, starting it off with pieces of paper on which some squares were drawn, then putting layers of the special wood and charcoal, and on top a mixture of nutmeg, cinnamon, incense, and the dried and powdered blood of a white goat.

They had to wait for the first night of a new moon to light the fire, and while they were waiting Aquil Khan cast the horoscopes of his two assistants to make sure that there were no bad planetary influences that might spoil the work. The fire had to be kept burning for four days and nights before it was used. The alchemist put a stone and a small lump of silver in one of the bowls he had made, and covered them with the dandelion sap. He then put the other bowl on top of the first and bound the two together with long strips of cotton dipped in clay. At every stage of the operation he kept looking at the stars, like a man consulting a watch. The bowl remained in the center of the fire

Right: the most important and traditional application of the system of magical correspondences was in alchemy. This 17th-century picture shows the four philosophers Geber, Aristotle, Rhozes, and Hermes guiding the work of four alchemists below. From the *Theatrum Chemicum Britannicum*, Bodleian Library, Oxford. MS Ashmole 971, f.36 verso.

for seven days and nights. When it was removed, cooled and the two halves prised apart, there was a nugget of yellow metal. A jeweler later confirmed that it was pure gold and offered to buy it. At the conclusion of the process Aquil told the woman: "It took me 30 years to learn this; 30 years of water and nuts, berries and starvation, contemplation and experiment. I had to learn to read the heavens, tame animals, read signs."

The Afghan's account of his art is similar to accounts by European alchemists. There is the same emphasis on purification, contemplation, and years of dedication to work. There is the hint that powers drawn down from the heavens bring about the magical transmutation. There is the statement that knowledge of signs is an essential part of the work.

The 16th-century German alchemist Oswald Crollius published a volume under the title *The Book of Signatures, or True and Vital Anatomy of the Greater and Lesser Worlds* in which he demonstrated that everything in the natural world carries the signature of the cosmic force with which it is linked. He maintained that the initiate who knows how to read signs can see at a glance the sympathies and antipathies between things, and learn their secret properties. It was precisely such knowledge that the Afghan alchemist claimed to practice.

The literature of alchemy contains many stories of successful transmutations of metals, not all of them easy to dismiss. We know that transmutation of the elements can and does take place through making changes in their atomic structure, and that such changes can only take place at extremely high temperatures. We also know that the art of the alchemist culminated in the act of drawing the forces of the heavens into the material world.

There is a good deal of evidence in the world that ancient man knew of technologies that baffle even the scientists of our highly technological age. For example, in 1960 archeologists found in China the grave of a general who had lived in the 3rd century A.D. In it were objects made of alloys that could not be made today, and that would require a very high temperature for their production. There were also aluminum objects. Until then it had been thought that man had only known how to make aluminum for about a century. Another instance of early technological knowledge is in Delhi, India. An ancient column of iron there, probably made between 376-414 A.D., does not corrode. These are but two of numerous inexplicable phenomena that make it difficult to dismiss the claims of alchemists, and suggest that magic may be a forgotten science or technology.

Ficino's sympathetic or natural magic was based on the belief that throughout the universe there exists a very fine and subtle substance which conducts the stellar and cosmic influences down to earth. He called this substance the *spiritus mundi*, or spirit of the world.

Right: by the middle of the 19th century when the British artist William Fettes Douglas painted this picture entitled *The Alchemist*, alchemy itself had fallen into almost total disrepute. But the figure of the alchemist himself was still that of a fabulous and wise old man, who was acquainted with secrets of supernatural power.

Above: Franz Mesmer studied medicine, but came to his theory of animal magnetism via astrology and a search for the method by which the stars affected humans. At first he thought the force was electricity rather than magnetism.

Left: an anonymous caricature of Mesmer and two of his supporters being struck by a thunderbolt from Aesculapius, the protector of traditional medicine. The three are seized by the guard dog of the underworld, who drags them down "to make them suffer the fate due to their ignorance." Meanwhile, the mesmerized woman who lies helplessly at the feet of Aesculapius is to be rescued by the minions of the irate god. Mesmer was often denounced as a fraud, and by the time he died he had been largely discredited.

In Ficino's day only two states of matter were known, liquids and solids. It was the 17th-century alchemist Johann Baptist van Helmont who discovered that matter can exist in a state thinner than fluidity, namely as a gas. Since his day many scientists have wondered whether there might not be yet another state of matter. Then, about 30 years ago, plasma was discovered. In technical language plasma is a gas that has had the electrons stripped off the nuclei of its atoms, and has become ionized. But its properties are greatly different from those of gas. It is a superconductor of electricity. It can reach temperatures of millions of degrees. It is luminous. Its energy can be contained and directed by a magnetic field. Most of the matter outside the earth's surface is plasma. In the light of these recent discoveries, Ficino's idea of a subtle substance that conducts stellar influences, the *spiritus mundi*, looks prophetic.

In the 1780s the fashionable people of Paris were flocking to

a clinic where there were some queer goings-on. They sat in a tub filled with a mixture of water and iron filings. From the tub protruded iron rods which, from time to time, those under treatment applied to the parts of their anatomy that were giving them trouble. Their therapist, dressed in a lilac gown, wielded a long magnet that he would point at his patients or touch them with. They might then form a chain—men and women alternating—and press their thighs against each other. Some remarkable cures were reported—which is perhaps not surprising in the light of what we now know about psychosomatic illnesses and the therapeutic value of getting rid of inhibitions. But it is the theory behind the therapy that is particularly interesting, the theory formulated by Franz Anton Mesmer, the gentleman in the lilac gown.

Mesmer's theory was that there is an invisible fluid that passes through everything in the universe, including the human body, and through which the influence of the planets is transmitted. He called this invisible fluid "animal magnetism." It was also known as "etheric fluid" or "psychic fluid." The human, he believed, is like a magnet with opposite poles on the left and right sides of the body. Disease is caused either by an imbalance of the animal magnetism, or obstructions to its circulation. Illness could therefore be cured by applying magnetic forces to move the fluid in the body so as to restore a correct balance between the poles. At first Mesmer used actual magnets in his experiments. Later he claimed that he could transmit animal magnetism from himself to his patient simply by stroking the patient and bringing on some sort of bodily convulsion. He was, in fact, not the first healer to use magnetic therapy. Paracelsus had claimed to cure epilepsy by checking the flow of fluid to the brain. He did this by placing the negative

Above: an anonymous engraving showing Mesmer at work among his patients (he is the one holding the magnet at the right of the tub). Two musicians play in the adjoining room to add to the atmosphere. Most of the time Mesmer's treatment consisted of bathing in the magnetized water, but he also used his magnet to touch the afflicted parts of the patient's body in an attempt to reestablish the correct balance within that individual's system.

Right: during the 1890s in Paris, Albert de Rochas hypnotized subjects who were then able to distinguish colored rays emitted from the human body, as shown in this illustration from his book. Using Mesmer's theory that the body has two poles, they reported that generally the north pole appeared to produce blue rays, and the south pole red ones —although this was not invariable.

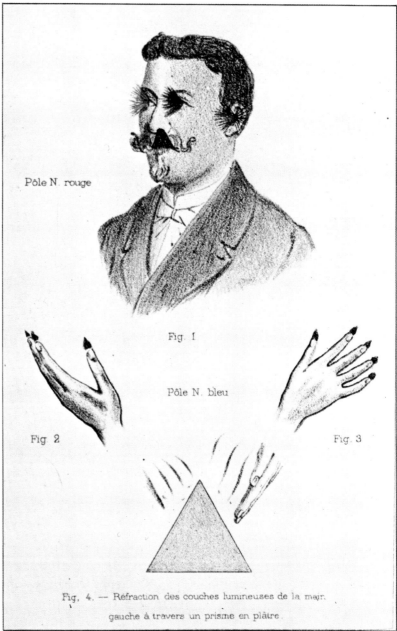

Pôle N. rouge

Fig. I

Pôle N. bleu

Fig 2

Fig. 3

Fig. 4. — Réfraction des couches lumineuses de la main gauche à travers un prisme en plâtre.

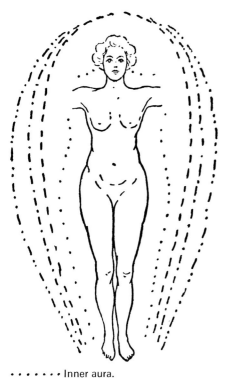

· · · · · · Inner aura.

— — — — Outer aura, when not well.

—·—·—·— Outer aura, when in good health.

—··—··— Outer aura, after electrifying positively.

Above: the aura as defined by Dr. Walter Kilner. He observed the aura through special colored glass. Although it was the Spiritualists who gave his work the warmest welcome, Kilner was emphatic that his ideas were not metaphysical, and not founded on occult principles or clairvoyance of any kind. He had been educated as a conventional medical doctor, and to his death firmly insisted that his work was purely scientific.

pole of a magnet on a patient's head, and the positive pole on the stomach. He had also used magnets in treating other ailments, apparently with success. Mesmer's successes, too, were spectacular, though how much they owed to the power of suggestion is difficult to assess.

Cranky and comical though his methods were, Mesmer's theories for a time exerted a great influence, and all over Europe people went around magnetizing each other, animals, and plants. It seemed to be an amiable and pleasant occupation, and in some cases, also a beneficial one. A Dr. Picard accelerated the growth and flowering of a rose bush by magnetizing it daily for five minutes morning and evening, and made one branch of a peach tree produce fruit more abundantly and earlier than others on the tree. The stories of the experiments of the magnetizers make fascinating reading, but what concerns

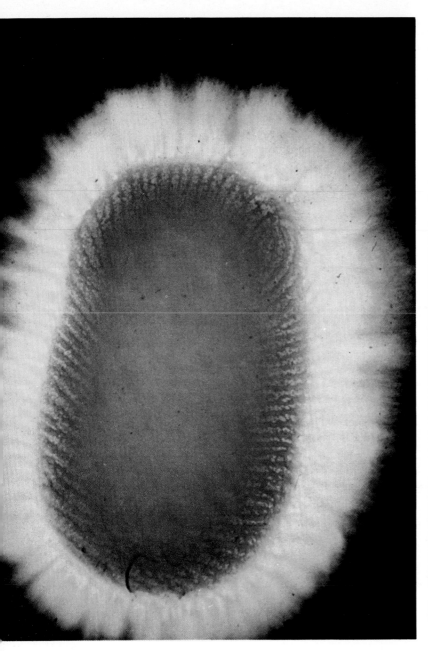

Left: Kirlian photography, which by use of long radio waves reveals that living things—plants and animals—have a pattern of flares surrounding them. The process was invented by Semyon and Valentina Kirlian working in South Russia. This picture of the fingertip of a healthy human being shows the luminous gas around it. Curiously, when illness strikes, the "aura" shows the earliest signs of change and irregularity.

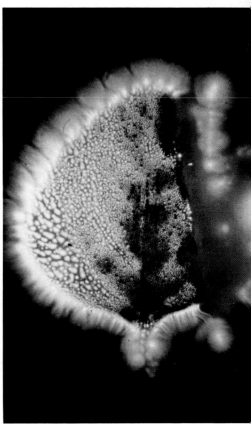

us here is Mesmer's theory behind the experiments. He believed that animal magnetism or psychic fluid is the invisible link between man and the cosmos through which man emits a kind of energy that can affect other organisms, and even the world of matter.

The 19th-century French writer on magic Eliphas Lévi declared boldly that "Mesmer rediscovered the secret science of Nature." He identified Mesmer's animal magnetism or psychic fluid with the "astral light," which is "either latent or active in all created substances." He quoted in support of his idea the 4th-century poet Synesius who said: "A single source, a single root of light, jets out and spreads itself into three branches of splendor. A breath blows around the earth, and vivifies in innumerable forms all parts of animated substance." Allowing for the poeticism, this seems to be much like a definition of recently

Above: a rose leaf with a portion cut away is seen to go on emitting its entire aura. This "phantom" aura lasts for about 15 minutes.

Below: an ordinary photograph of a healthy leaf from a geranium. Bottom: a Kirlian photograph of the leaf showing its surrounding aura. At this stage the aura is of bluish flares that glow strongly and evenly in a flashing pattern around the tips of the entire leaf.

discovered plasma. So, too, is Lévi's definition of the astral light as both a force and a substance, for plasma, though intangible and invisible, has the metallic properties of responding to magnetism and conducting electricity.

Since Mesmer's day, numerous researchers have sought to demonstrate the existence of the etheric or psychic fluid. Between 1845 and 1868 the German chemist Karl Reichenbach published several books demonstrating the existence in all matter and all organisms of a natural energy that he called *od*. His evidence was the testimony of a number of sensitives (people with sharper sense perceptions than usual) who, if kept in the dark for an hour or more, could see gleams of light like flames emitted from the poles of magnets, from crystals, and in some cases from the fingers of a human hand. They also felt sensations of heat and cold in connection with these lights.

In 1891 a Colonel de Rochas and a Dr. Luys began a series of experiments in Paris developing Reichenbach's work. They used hypnotized subjects. In 1912 an Englishman, Dr. Walter Kilner, published the results of a long series of experiments. By looking through colored glass screens he found that he could see a radiant fringe or aura about six inches wide around most bodies. He claimed that this visible aura was in three distinct layers, and varied with the age, sex, mental abilities, and health of the

subject. He also believed that it could be used as an aid to medical diagnosis. In 1921 a French researcher, Du Bourg de Bozas, produced photographic evidence that certain psychic subjects could emit from their hands a "tube of fluidic force" that would penetrate a sheet of lead five centimeters thick. Another Frenchman, Boirac, discovered that he could anesthetize an area of a person's body simply by pointing his hand at it. A blindfolded subject would be able to describe sensations of touch on all parts of his body except the area that the experimenter was pointing at. Two doctors in Bordeaux conducted many experiments with a woman who could halt natural processes such as the fermentation of wine and the decay of animal organs by holding her hands over them. She apparently emitted some energy that was lethal for bacteria, and was able permanently to mummify the corpses of birds and small animals by means of that unusual energy.

In recent years research into human energy fields has become more sophisticated and more scientifically controlled. The process known as Kirlian photography has demonstrated that all living things emit vivid patterns of light and color, which are not visible under normal conditions. For example, a leaf or hand placed in the middle of two plates, between which a high-frequency electrical field is passed, are seen to have an aura of

Bottom: the same geranium leaf after it has been deprived of light for 72 hours. The shape of the aura has become rounded, and a reddish color has spread over the center. Below: the dead leaf. The outer flashes have been extinguished and the leaf is almost completely red.

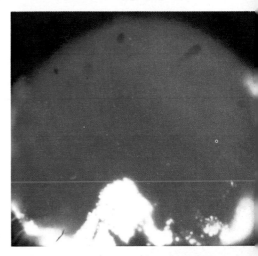

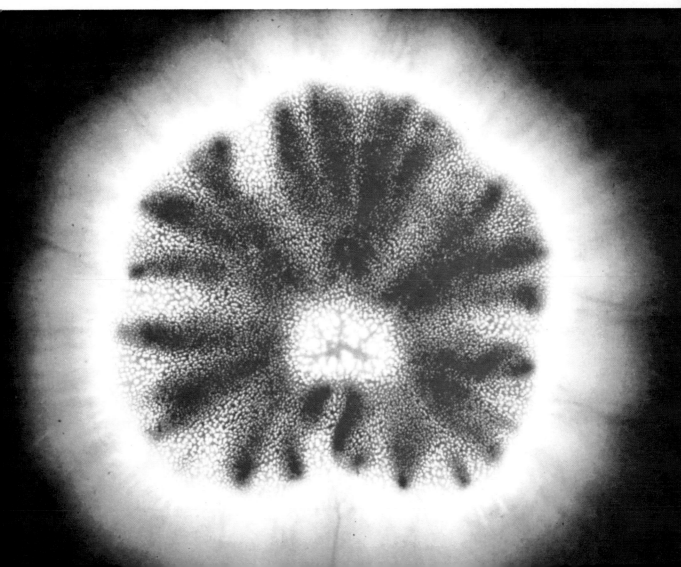

Charles Leadbeater and the Human Aura

For C. W. Leadbeater, the world was a wonderfully complex place, containing much more than was ordinarily visible. This English clergyman became a leading figure in the Theosophical Society, which believed in and explored the invisible spirit world unknown to most of us. By using clairvoyance, he believed that a greater reality was available to all of mankind.

In no way was this greater reality more obvious to Leadbeater than in the aura which he saw surrounding each person. According to him, this aura was an emanation of the astral body, and gave a key to peoples' state of spiritual development and individual temperament. It was clearly visible to the trained clairvoyant, Leadbeater said. The savage or an uncivilized man will have a weak and pale-colored aura, but the developed man or woman—described as "a seeker after the higher truth" —will have a finely colored aura. This expresses capacity to serve as a channel for the higher force. Such people are possessed of a crown of brilliant sparks that rise from the upper part of the body, adding greatly to their dignity. This sparkling aura surrounds them whatever they might be doing with their physical body

light with vivid flares streaming from the pores. Healing by touch, or the laying on of hands, has long been practiced all over the world, and now Kirlian photography has shown that the emissions from the fingers of a healer are of exceptional intensity and length.

Until quite recently acupuncture—the ancient Chinese practice of sticking needles into the body to prevent and cure diseases— was regarded by many in the West as strange and unscientific. Now, through Kirlian photography, an exact correspondence has been discovered between the points where the body gives off its most intense emissions of light and color, and the points where the acupuncturists stick their needles. In 1973 an American book reported the proceedings of a conference on "the human aura in acupuncture and Kirlian photography." It said that "the function of the acupuncture stimulation was primarily to take energy out of one limb of the circuit and put it into another—to shift these energies around so that one obtained a balanced system." This is remarkably similar to Mesmer's idea that disease can be cured by shifting the etheric fluid in the body, and restoring a balance between the magnetic poles. The title of this American book, *Galaxies of Life*, serves to remind us that all these developments in the sciences come back to the central theme of the hermetic philosophy and of magical traditions: as above, so below. Kirlian photographs of the energy fields of living organisms have a striking and weird resemblance to pictures of astronomical formations and constellations, such as the milky way, the spiral and crab nebulae of distant galaxies, and solar flares.

Color healing is not new. In Heliopolis in ancient Egypt there were temples of light and color that were used for purposes of therapy. Present-day enthusiasts claim that perfect health can be insured, and even the severest diseases can be cured, by applying knowledge of the principles and functions of light and color. Techniques for breathing certain colors, for bathing in them, or for absorbing them through specified food and drinks are prescribed by Dr. Roland Hunt in his book *The Seven Keys to Color Healing*, published in 1971. Dr. Hunt, like Dr. Kilner 60 years ago, claims that illness can be diagnosed by observing the condition of and the colors in the etheric aura that surrounds the human body. His treatments involve the use of metals as well as breathing, diet, and exposure to light. He declares that red radiations can be absorbed from iron, yellow from gold, green from copper, and blue from tin. A glance at the table on page 28 will show that these are the same correspondences handed down in magical lore.

Orthodox scientists and doctors may scoff at the idea of the human aura or energy body, but magicians and psychic healers down the centuries and throughout the world have produced a body of remarkably consistent testimony for its existence. Magicians claim that their powers come from the etheric or astral plane, and that their art consists in knowing how to channel a stream of astral light into and through the body. The recognition of the magical patterns of correspondences between man, nature, and the cosmos is an important introduction to how practical magic is actually done.

These illustrations, showing the effect that various emotions have on the aura as seen clairvoyantly, are from the book *Man Visible and Invisible* published in 1907. It was by C. W. Leadbeater, who wrote widely on occult subjects. In his view the true shape of the mental and astral material around the physical body is roughly ovoid.

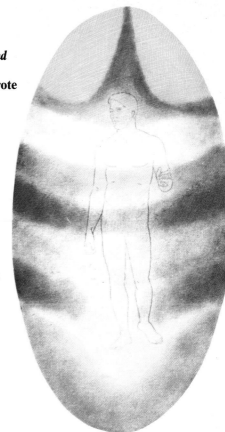

Top left: the astral body when convulsed with fear. Terror will "in an instant suffuse the entire body with a curious livid gray mist," according to Leadbeater.

Top right: the calm scientific man. The large quantity of golden yellow at the top shows a well-developed intelligence, and the orange cone rising through the yellow shows there is justifiable pride and ambition in connection with the knowledge indicated. The scientific and orderly habit of mind has an obvious effect upon the astral colors, which fall into neat and regular bands.

Below left: the irritable man. His astral body is filled with small floating scarlet specks showing outbursts of temper over the vexations of ordinary life. Some flecks are cast out in the direction of the person assumed to be responsible for whatever has gone wrong, but many remain floating around in his astral body. Although they gradually fade away, there is likely to be a continuous source of new ones as the irritable man finds new subjects for his annoyance.

Below right: the angry man. The faint outline of the man is almost hidden by the heavy, thunderous masses of sooty blackness as the man gives way to a fit of passion. Fiery arrows of rage shoot through the black, and the terrible flashes penetrate other astral bodies like swords. Therefore, though he may be able to restrain himself from giving way to physical violence, he is nonetheless injuring others on the astral plane.

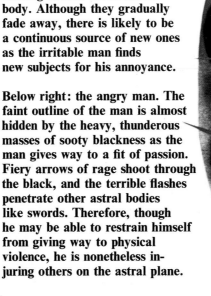

Mysteries of the Cabala

Above: a 16th-century woodcut of a Jewish cabalist holding the Tree of Life. The Tree is visualized as growing downward with its roots above. The circles give the Hebrew name for each of the sefira. Together the sefiroth —or 10 aspects of the Divine— are seen as making up God's name.

Right: a modern artist, Godfrey Dawson, produced this image of the sefiroth. He drew freely on all the elements which have come to enrich the cabalist tradition.

There is a legend that God whispered the secret wisdom of the Cabala to Moses on Mount Sinai, that Moses communicated it to the 70 elders, and that they in turn passed it on to their immediate successors. It remained a secret, oral tradition known to very few until centuries later, when various anonymous authors began to write down their different versions. There are those who maintain that even today the most profound truths of the Cabala are known to only a handful of initiates. They are passed on either by word of mouth or through closely guarded, ancient, unpublished manuscripts to those who have proved themselves

49

"Worthy of a lifetime's study and contemplation"

especially worthy of carrying on this mystical tradition.

Cabala is a Hebrew word that means knowledge or tradition. It is used to refer to a large body of mystical speculation that includes writings by many authors, and that spans many centuries. Among the vast amount of literature two books stand out as the most important. One is the *Sefer Yetzirah* or Book of Creation, which was probably written in Palestine or Babylon between the 3rd and 6th centuries A.D. The other is known as the *Zohar* or Book of Splendor, and was probably written in Spain in the late 13th century by Moses de Léon.

The ideas of the Cabala have much in common with those of gnosticism, which also flourished in the countries of the Eastern Mediterranean around the time of Christ. *Gnosis* means knowledge of spiritual things obtained by divine inspiration. Unlike the Christians, who believed that the road to salvation was through faith, love, and good deeds, cabalists and gnostics held that it was only possible to reach God through knowledge. They believed that the chosen were those who had obtained this knowledge, and that we are cut off from God not by sin in the Christian sense, but by ignorance.

The tradition of the Cabala is predominantly Jewish, but since the Renaissance humanists, philosophers, psychologists, and occultists have seized on it with enthusiasm. Each have extracted from its great diversity and richness those features that best fit in with their particular scheme of thought. The Cabala is in some ways the *I Ching* of the West, worthy of a lifetime's study and contemplation. It is complex and inexhaustible, but at the same time accessible in its basic conceptions.

Magicians and occultists have, of course, been attracted by the mystery and secrecy surrounding the Cabala. But they have also found themselves in sympathy with many of its underlying beliefs. Common both to the Cabala and to occultists is the idea that all things in the Universe are part of an organized whole, governed by secret laws, and with hidden connections or correspondences between many things that do not overtly appear to be linked. Shared, too, is the notion that all phenomena contain something of the divine, and that man is, in some way and on a minute scale, a reflection of both God and the Universe. The idea of a path that we can climb in stages to reach God is fundamental both to the Cabala and to theories of magic throughout the centuries.

Behind the cabalist system of thought is the basic doctrine that God is completely unknowable. He cannot even be directly addressed in prayer. He is everything and nothing. He cannot be ascribed qualities of good and evil. He is known as *En Sof*, Infinite Radiance. He did not create the Universe, and therefore cannot be responsible for it. The Universe emanated or flowed out from Him. According to the *Zohar*, a single ray of light burst out from the closed confines of En Sof, and from this light came nine further lights. This process of emanation was the way in which the unknowable God revealed certain aspects of Himself. Each of the ten lights can be seen both as facets of God and as stages in His revelation of Himself. They are known as the *sefiroth* (one light is a *sefira*), and are seen as constituting God's name because they are the identity that he has revealed.

Below: a miniature of Moses from a medieval Bible. In spite of the tradition that Moses received the secrets of the Cabala while on Mount Sinai, it seems clear that what we now call the Cabala grew out of the Merkabah or "Throne" mysticism of Judaism. This flourished from the 4th to 10th centuries in the Middle East.

Right: one unorthodox form of Christianity which had much in common with Cabalism was the heresy Gnosticism. In the 12th century, a Gnostic sect known as the Cathars arose in Europe and was savagely repressed. Here St. Dominic is shown burning Cathar books. One "pure" book rises, untouched, from the flames consuming the rest.

Below: an 18th-century Gnostic charm showing the "Savior of the World," a common Gnostic figure.

The 10 sefiroth are regarded as underlying the construction of the Universe and of man, both of which are in the image of God. They are also the forces behind man and the Universe. There are 22 paths connecting the 10 sefiroth to each other. As we shall see later, the 10 sefiroth, each of which has its own name, are linked to the numbers 1 to 10, and the 22 paths are linked to the 22 letters of the Hebrew alphabet. The sefiroth and paths are usually depicted by circles and lines in the Tree of Life, and this Tree embraces and classifies everything in the Universe. This is shown at the top on page 53.

The Tree of Life also shows how God descended in a flash from *Kether*, the first emanation or Crown, through the sefiroth to *Malkhuth*, the Earth or the Earthly Kingdom. To reach God

51

the soul has to make the journey in reverse through the sefiroth, a long and arduous climb beset with many pitfalls. This route is shown at the bottom of this page.

The idea of the Tree of Life has much in common with the widely held belief in the construction of the Universe that existed from classical times right up to the 16th century. This stated that the Universe was made up of nine concentric spheres. God was accorded the outer sphere, the stars made up the second sphere, and each of the planets then known were alloted one of the next seven spheres. Of these, the moon was the innermost sphere. It contained the earth, which was not considered a separate sphere. Cabalists were influenced by Pythagorean theories based on the numbers 1 to 10. In order to make the planetary spheres correspond with the 10 sefiroth and the first 10 numbers, they increased the spheres in this scheme to 10, making the earth a sphere on its own to correspond with Malkuth or Earth on the Tree of Life. The seven sefiroth above Malkuth correspond with the seven planets; *Hokmah* or Divine Wisdom with the sphere of the stars or zodiac; and Kether, the Crown, with God.

In the early centuries after Christ, the idea of the soul's descent and ascent through the spheres took shape in the countries of the Eastern Mediterranean. This idea was absorbed by the cabalists and adapted to the Tree of Life. It was believed that the human soul originated in God and descended through the spheres, picking up the characteristic of each like a new skin as it passed through. For example, from Venus it took love and from Mercury it took intelligence. Finally it reached the earth and added the last layer or skin, the physical body. It was now a miniature image of the Universe, each layer corresponding to a sphere, or sefira in cabalistic terminology. This idea is the clearest illustration of the cabalist belief that man is a reflection of both the Universe and God.

Once in the body, the soul longed to return to its origin, to go back up through the spheres and be reunited with God. It could begin its ascent at the moment of death. But the way was difficult and hazardous because each sefira was guarded by angels that would try to prevent the soul from continuing. The lower spheres were also full of evil spirits that would try to ensnare unwary souls. The soul's progress would depend on the knowledge it had gained in life of the secrets of each sphere, and of how to overcome its guardian angels. It can be seen clearly that knowledge, rather than a pious life, was all-important for the progress of the soul, although there have doubtless been many pious and religious cabalists. Cabalists also believed that the soul might begin its ascent before death through the mastery of certain techniques and knowledge. It is probably mostly this belief that attracted

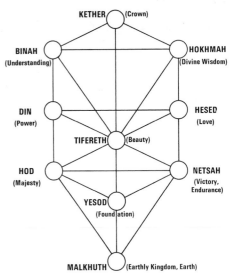

Above: the 10 sefiroth with the 22 pathways connecting them. The sefiroth shown here are the emanations of En Sof, the totally unknowable, uncomprehensible God. The ten sefirothic lights are grouped in three triads. The first is Kether, Hokmah, and Binah, and they represent the thought process of God. The second triad is Hesed, Din, and Tifereth, symbolic of God's moral power. The third triad is Netsah, Hod, and Yesod, the material universe. At the bottom is Malkuth, the earth, where the paths all begin.

Below: the lightning flash by which God descended from Kether to Malkuth to create Adam Kadmon, the metaphysical counterpart of the biblical first man, Adam.

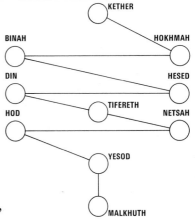

Left: an illustration from the 15th-century work *Opera Chemica* by Raymond Lull, showing the Hermetic philosophy of Nature. At the center of the picture is the Serpent of Wisdom, twined around the Tree of Life. The Hermetic works are a religious and philosophical literature of about the 1st century B.C. to the 2nd century A.D. about a great Egyptian god Hermes Trismegistus, the "thrice-greatest."

53

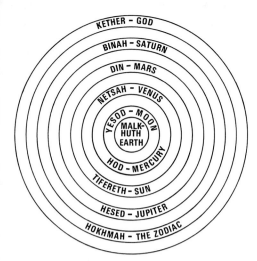

KETHER – GOD
BINAH – SATURN
DIN – MARS
NETSAH – VENUS
YESOD – MOON
MALK-HUTH EARTH
HOD – MERCURY
TIFERETH – SUN
HESED – JUPITER
HOKHMAH – THE ZODIAC

magicians as well as religious and other mystics to the Cabala.

The correspondence between the sefiroth on the Tree of Life and the planetary spheres is shown even more clearly when the sefiroth are represented, as they sometimes are, by 10 concentric spheres. In the diagram on the left the planetary correspondence for each sefira has been given in order to make the link clearer. When the Cabala is used as a basis for magical operations, it is essential to know the planetary association of each sefira in order to make use of the appropriate symbols and system of correspondences.

Illustrating the sefiroth as concentric spheres clearly shows that, because the spheres decrease in power and dignity as they reduce in size, it takes an immense expansion of consciousness for each stage of the journey by the soul from the inner circle to the outer. Outside of showing this, the Tree is a much more suggestive and versatile representation. It can be contemplated in different ways, various patterns within it can be focused and, with the exercise of a little imagination, everything in the Universe can be fitted into it and assigned to one or another of the sefira. It is, as Aleister Crowley said, like a great card-index file.

The Ptolemaic concept of the Universe (below) was the only one accepted from ancient Greek times to the 16th century. Yet it is based on the same thinking as the concept of the cabalists (above).

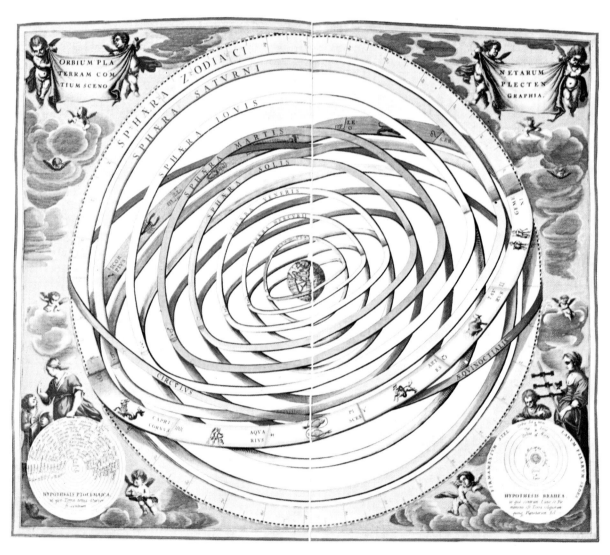

Our understanding of the sefiroth and the relationship between them may be increased by looking at them in different groupings. They are sometimes thought of by cabalists as forming three pillars, as in the diagram on page 58. Those on the right side of the tree bring together the male, positive, light principles of the Universe (like the Yang of Chinese philosophy). Hokmah is the father of the Universe, the force behind everything active, creative, and changing. *Hesed* or Love, is the force that civilizes and governs, the merciful loving father, the guide and protector. *Netsah* or Victory and Endurance, at the base of the male pillar, represents the force of Nature, of human instincts, impulses, and emotions. These three male sefiroth together make up the Pillar of Mercy.

On the left side of the tree are the three sefiroth that represent the female, passive, dark principles (like the Yin). At the top is *Binah* or Understanding, the mother of the Universe, passive and receptive until fertilized, and then prolific. Binah represents slumbering potentiality and all-embracing understanding. It is the stable counterpart to the dynamic Hokmah at the head of the male pillar. The counterpart to the loving merciful Hesed is *Din* or Power (also known as *Geburah*), standing for severity and discipline. Din is the force that destroys, whereas Hesed builds. But it also stands for energy and realism. At the bottom of the female pillar is *Hod* or Majesty, the counterpart of the male Netsah. Where Netsah stands for animal instincts and emotions, Hod represents the higher powers of the mind such as intuition and inspiration. These three female sefiroth form the Pillar of Severity.

Reconciling the male and female pillars is the Pillar of Equilibrium. It is also known as the Pillar of the Soul or of Consciousness. The *Zohar* calls it the perfect pillar, mediating between the forces of light and darkness, but not dependent on them for existence. At the top of the pillar is Kether, the first emanation of the unknowable Godhead or Divinity. Then comes *Tifereth* or Beauty, and *Yesod* or Foundation. Yesod is connected with mystery and magical power. Finally, at the base is Malkhuth, the Earth.

Another way of looking at the sefiroth is in terms of three triangles with Malkhuth, the 10th sefira, at the bottom. Each triangle will contain two opposing forces from the male and female pillars, and one reconciling force from the central pillar. The top triangle of Kether, Hokmah, and Binah or Divinity, Wisdom, and Understanding, represents the ideal intellectual world. The next triangle of Tifereth, Hesed, and Din or Beauty, Mercy, and Power, represents the actual moral world, and the third triangle of Yesod, Netsah, and Hod, or Foundation, Victory, and Majesty, represents the astral or magical world.

The parts of the Tree of Life are upside down in comparison to a real tree. Kether, at the top, represents the roots of the Tree. The branches containing the other sefiroth spread and grow downward. Another common way to portray the sefiroth is in the form of a man, this time the right way up, with Kether representing the head. The first three sefiroth are the three cavities of the brain, the fourth and fifth are the arms, the sixth the torso, and the seventh and eighth the legs. The ninth represents the sexual organs, and

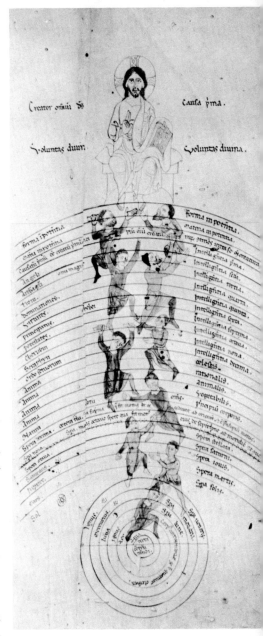

Above: in the Hermetic version of the soul's progress toward God, the soul spiraled its way through the spheres which—as in cabalistic thought—reversed the original process of creation. This illustration comes from an anonymous 12th-century Hermetic manuscript; but the Hermetic tradition itself dates from around the time of Christ, a period of profound civil uproar and ideological chaos—the period in which Gnosticism and Cabalism were also taking shape. Mysteries and magic fascinated philosophers.

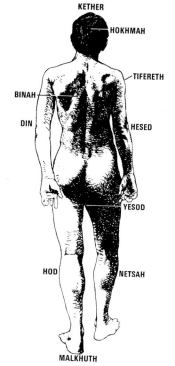

KETHER
HOKHMAH
TIFERETH
BINAH
DIN
HESED
YESOD
HOD
NETSAH
MALKHUTH

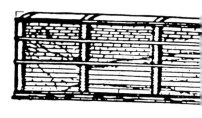

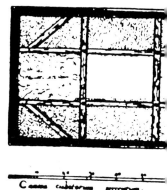

Left: the cabalist conception of Adam Kadmon, the Heavenly or Primordial Man. Some cabalists are of the opinion that the first form patterned by the En Sof was not the sefiroth, but the body of Adam Kadmon (of which Adam in Eden is the Old Testament counterpart). Adam Kadmon is traditionally shown from the rear because in the Book of Exodus when Moses on the Mount asks God to show him His Glory, the reply is, "Thou shalt see my back parts: but my face shall not be seen."

Right: Noah and his Ark represented astronomically. The 10 compartments correspond to 10 of the signs of the zodiac. Such a tie-in with astrology stems mainly from Christian cabalistic beliefs.

אדם קדמון שני
עתיק יומין
אריך
אנפין

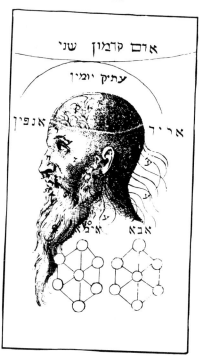

Above: the head of Adam Kadmon, from a 17th-century cabalistic text. When, as shown here, Kether is personified as the head, it is always shown in profile to accord with the cabalistic statement that Adam is partially hidden.

the tenth either the total image of man or, in a different interpretation, woman.

The correspondences and attributes of the sefiroth are sometimes unexpected. Many of the qualities that we normally think of as being masculine appear in the female sefiroth, and vice versa. Planetary association too are not immediately obvious. But the Cabala has its own fascinating logic. For example, Binah, the female force behind everything stable and potential, is linked to the planet Saturn, the planet of stability, old age, and fate. Netsah, the male force behind nature, animal drives, and passions, is linked to Venus, the goddess of sensuality and nature. All the sefiroth are rich in imagery and association, which is especially important when the Cabala is used for magical purposes.

Kether, the Crown, is the first emanation and corresponds with the number 1. The soul that reaches this sefira achieves union with God. It is guarded by the creatures described in the first chapter of *Ezekiel*: "and everyone had four faces, and everyone had four wings." Its symbols are the point, which stands for 1, and the crown. When meditating on Kether the cabalist must concentrate on the image of an old bearded man seen in profile.

Hokmah, Wisdom, is the father of the Universe. It is the next emanation from Kether and therefore its number is 2. Because it is the force behind activity, its guardian angels are the Wheels in *Ezekiel*, which moved around and had the spirit of life in them. Hokmah's symbols are the phallus, the tower, and the straight line, and the image to be used in contemplation is a bearded man.

Binah, Understanding, is the mother of the Universe. Being the third emanation, it is associated with the number 3. Its symbols are the female genitals, the cup, the circle, the diamond, and the oval. As with the other female sefiroth, Binah has conflicting attributes—of life and death, of goodness and evil. It is associated both with the mother goddesses and with Hecate,

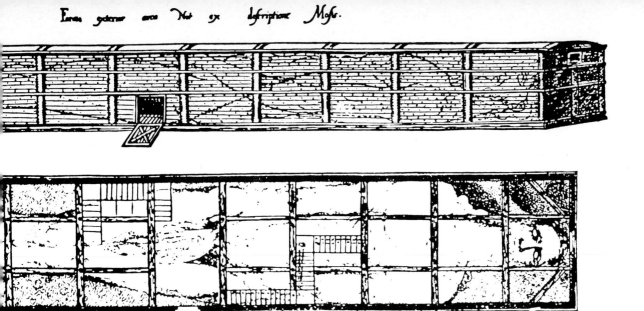

goddess of witchcraft and sorcery. Its image for contemplation is a mature woman.

Hesed, Love, is accorded number 4, and is the male force that organizes and builds things up. Its symbols are the king's scepter, the magician's wand, and the bishop's crook, as well as the Greek cross (+) and the pyramid. It is linked to the unicorn, which stands for virility and power, and its image for contemplation is a powerful king on a throne.

Din, Power, is number 5 and the female counterpart of Hesed. It lies behind all destruction, hatred, and war. Its planet is Mars and its symbols are the sword, spear, scourge, chain, and the pentagon, which is linked with the number five. Many cabalists see Din as the source of evil. There is even a theory that its destructive energy overflowed and created its own Tree of evil emanations. Din is associated with the mythical basilisk, a fierce deadly creature. Its image for contemplation is a warrior in a chariot.

Tifereth, Beauty, is number 6, and linked to the sphere of the sun. It is vital energy, and it balances the destructive and constructive forces of Din and Hesed. Christian cabalists associate Tifereth with Christ, both because of its direct descent from Kether, which stands for God, and because the sun had an early symbolic association with Christ. Tifereth can be represented by a lion, the beast of the sun, or by a phoenix or child, the symbols of immortality and mortality. Its images for contemplation are a majestic king and a sacrificed child.

Netsah, Victory, is number 7, the male force behind nature. It stands for the senses and passions. It is the sefira of the arts and of rhythm, movement, and color. Its sphere is Venus, and the bird associated with it, the wryneck, is used in love charms. Its image, again associated with Venus, is a beautiful naked woman.

Hod, Majesty, is number 8. It is the female force standing for the higher qualities of the mind, such as intuition and insight. But

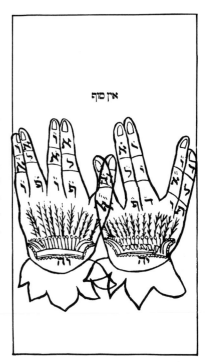

Above: in cabalistic writings, a system of symbolic correspondences was developed between the sefiroth and the parts of the body. Here, the hands have been divided into parts whose total equals the 10 sefiroth and 22 paths of the Cabala.

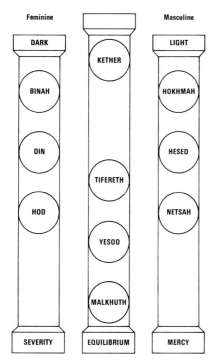

Feminine — Masculine

DARK — LIGHT

KETHER

BINAH — HOKHMAH

DIN — HESED

TIFERETH

HOD — NETSAH

YESOD

MALKHUTH

SEVERITY — EQUILIBRIUM — MERCY

Above: another way of looking at the sefiroth is to consider them as three pillars, which creates a whole new set of relationships. In this way the theme of opposites is emphasized, with the masculine sefiroth on the right-hand pillar, and the feminine on the left-hand. The middle pillar acts as a balance between them. This pillar in addition provides a direct line from the divine (Kether) to the material (Malkuth), which are the supreme cabalistic opposites.

it also stands for qualities of reason and logic, distrusted by the Cabala. Like the other feminine sefiroth, there is a conflict between good and evil. It stands for wisdom as well as trickery and cunning. Its planet is Mercury, the god of intelligence and magic, and the twin serpents from Mercury's wand are often associated with Hod. Likewise, its image for contemplation is a hermaphrodite, which is also a symbol for the metal mercury in alchemy.

Yesod, Foundation, is the ninth sefira and the basis of all active forces in God. It stands for creativity, both sexual and mental. When the sefiroth are depicted as a man, Yesod is shown as the genitals. Its number is 9, and 9 is the number of initiation into magic and the occult. Its sphere is the moon, and the moon is the planet of magic. Its reconciliation of the animal drives of Netsah and the intellectual faculties of Hod give it great potential magical power. It is associated with the elephant, the animal that combines strength and intelligence, and its image for contemplation is a beautiful naked man.

Malkhuth, the Earthly Kingdom, is the tenth sefira. The number 10 means "all things," and Malkhuth unites all the sefiroth in one somewhat like man is seen as uniting all the features of the planetary spheres. It is associated with the sphinx, which stands for the unity of heaven and earth. This sefira is also known as *Shekinah,* the bride of God. The purpose of the Cabala is to unite God, the first emanation, with His lost bride Shekinah, the tenth emanation or, put differently, to ascend from the tenth sefira to the first. The image for contemplation is a young woman, crowned and seated on a throne.

Ambiguities abound in the Cabala, particularly when we come to the lower sefiroth, for each sefira receives influences from others connected with it on horizontal, vertical, and diagonal planes. But ambiguities also abound in life, and cabalists believe that contemplation based on the Tree and its patterns may reveal more about life and the universe than any explicit and unambiguous philosophical statement could. The attributes of the sexes and the relations between them, for example, are certainly more ambiguous than commonly accepted patterns of thinking and living allow for. The contemplation of the structure and symbolism of the Cabala, therefore, could probably revitalize many an ailing marriage. Dion Fortune, who was the leading modern English cabalist, writes, "The Tree is a method of using the mind, not a system of knowledge." The fascination of the Cabala is that it leads the mind beyond ambiguities to profound truths and insights.

Magic too is a method of using the mind, or rather the powers of the mind. Aleister Crowley, the modern magician, defined magic as "the science and art of causing changes to occur in conformity with will." The cabalist who wished to make the journey through the sefiroth during his lifetime had to learn to detach himself from the physical world by mastering the powers of concentration and imagination. He learned to achieve a trancelike state in which he could visualize a clear image of his own body in front of him, like a double. He then had to transfer his consciousness to the second body so that he was functioning through it, and he was ready to begin the long hard ascent.

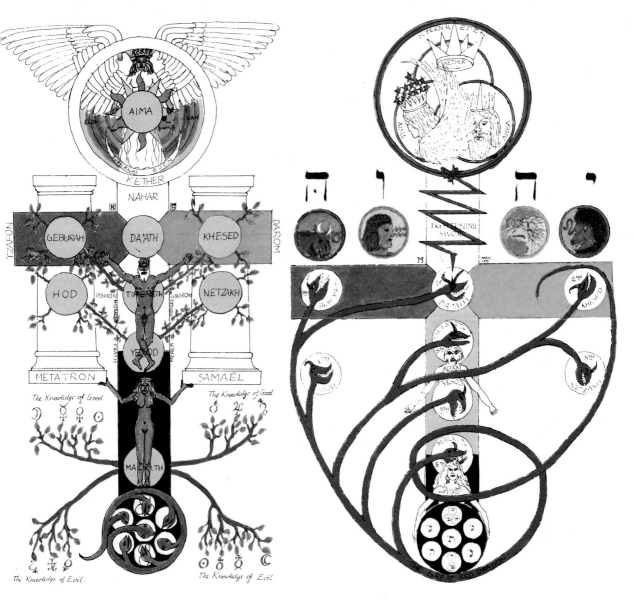

Modern magicians and occultists employ many of the same techniques as the cabalists, but they think of the journey through the sefiroth as a journey in the astral plane, another dimension of the world, and of the body on that plane as the astral body. The astral plane includes the ordinary world, but it extends beyond it to the realm where the products of thought and imagination have reality. The astral body is the spiritual replica of the physical body, and is able to travel through space and solid objects. In the Tree of Life, the gateway to the astral world is Yesod, which corresponds to the sphere of the Moon. It is the link between Earth and the rest of the Universe.

The Cabala has had a great influence on modern occultists and magicians. Eliphas Lévi, whose books are still widely read today, spent much time working on a theory of correspondences. He studied both the Cabala and the Tarot, that curious pack of fortune-telling cards of uncertain origin. Lévi related the 22 symbolic cards of the Tarot to the 22 letters of the Hebrew alphabet. These letters, as we have seen, are related to the 22

Above: two modern drawings, *The Garden of Eden Before* (left) and *After the Fall*, show how the story from Genesis, like other religious and mythic episodes, is enriched by cabalistic symbolism. Before, Adam and Eve are free and vigorous, Adam in Tifereth with his arms stretched out, and Eve in Malkuth, supporting the two great pillars. Below them the Serpent of Wisdom encircles the seven palaces, giving the key to paths on the Tree of Life. After the fall, the serpent has become the Red Dragon, the apocalyptic monster with eight heads and 11 horns and both Adam and Eve are caught hopelessly in the tangles.

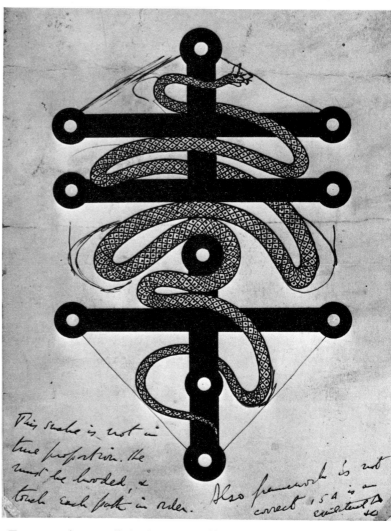

This snake is not in true proportion. the [...] he hooded, & touch each path in order. Also framework is not correct 15ª is an existent 16

paths of the Tree of Life. Thus the Tarot cards were linked to the Cabala.

Lévi's theories on correspondences were greatly expanded by the Order of the Golden Dawn, the magical society that flourished in England in the 1890s. With amazing thoroughness, members of the Golden Dawn elaborated one of the most complex and all-embracing systems of ritual magic. Mythologies and religions were combed and out of them Greek, Roman, and Egyptian gods, and Christian and Jewish spirits were apportioned among the sefiroth and the 22 paths. Colors, animals, stones, and scents were among the other objects and attributes that were classified. The magician who wished to find the appropriate ritual for each sefira could thereafter look it up in a Table of Correspondences.

The 22 connecting lines between the 10 sefiroth are called the Paths of Wisdom. According to Dion Fortune "the sefiroth are natural forces, the Paths states of consciousness." Each path represents an equilibrium between the forces of the two sefiroth it connects. Each is associated with a planet or zodiac sign, a color, certain plants, a symbolic Tarot card, and various animals and birds, among other things. It is by "working" the paths that the Tree is employed in meditation or magic. Working a path means visualizing intensely a trip along it while seeing all the

Above left: Aleister Crowley, who became the most notorious magician of the 20th century, shown here as a young man. He encountered the Cabala early in his life, and was profoundly influenced by its concepts.

Above: one of Crowley's cabalistic drawings, showing the way of the Serpent through the sefiroth, with Crowley's own notations.

Right: this modern painting of Aleister Crowley, repeating some of the symbolism that was so important in his work on magic, emphasizes the fascination that master magician still holds for many people. In life he possessed a magnetic attraction for some disciples. In death, his teachings still attract many new students.

things associated with it, such as scents, colors, plants, and creatures. Each sefira also has a negative aspect or *qlifah*, and there is a point in every magical operation when this negative force has to be dealt with and conquered.

The following description gives a good idea of how a modern magician might use the Cabala. A room will be suitably curtained and supplied with an altar, candles, a gong or gavel, and enough space for the magician to make some sweeping flourishes with his ritual sword. He begins by drawing the magic circle in which he is going to operate. This may be done with chalk or, in a carpeted room, with string or cotton. The circle keeps out evil forces, and in drawing it the magician leaves a gap to enter through when he has completed his preliminary preparations.

To the east of the circle the magician draws a triangle, the purpose of which is to confine any demonic or angelic being that is conjured up. These preparations completed, he puts out all lights except his altar candle, steps inside his circle, closes it, and drives all undesirable influences from the area by making the cabalistic cross. Standing in the middle of the circle, he visualizes a great cloud of light above his head. This is the light of Kether. Raising his right hand, he draws some of the light down to his forehead, then touches in turn his solar plexus, his right shoulder, and his left shoulder, saying "Malkhuth," "Din," and "Hesed" as he does so, and all the time visualizing the stream of ketheric light trailing from his finger. He is projecting his body onto the Tree of Life, and he imagines both the Tree and his body growing to a tremendous size so that he is standing above the Universe with the stars at his feet. Returning to his normal size, he next traces pentagrams in the air in front of him with his ritual sword, one for each of the four points of the compass. These pentagrams represent extra barriers against inimical forces, and are also his points of contact with the astral world. There is an archangel associated with each of them, and he greets these archangels— Raphael, Gabriel, Michael, and Uriel—with great compliments chanted in Latin. At the same time he visualizes them in all their splendor. Above his head he imagines a six-pointed star comprised of two interlaced triangles. These represent the fusion of his temporal physical self with the eternal cosmic forces.

Now the magician is ready to travel from Malkhuth, the earth, to Yesod, the gateway to the astral world and to the other sefiroth. He travels along path 22, the Path of Saturn. On the way he may well meet the Tarot symbol corresponding with this path, which is a naked young woman garlanded with flowers, carrying two wands, and dancing. This stands for joy, release from earthly concerns, and entry into the higher magical world. On the other hand he may meet a crocodile, the symbolic creature of Saturn. Arriving at the threshold of Yesod, he gains entry in the name of Gabriel and humbly confesses to the guardian angels his ignorance of the mysteries that surround him. He informs them which sefira he wishes to work with, and then proceeds from Yesod along the appropriate paths toward his destination. As he travels he visualizes around him all the creatures, plants, colors, and other attributes that he would expect to find on each particular path. Of this stage of the operation Dion Fortune writes: "To project the astral body

Right: the Tree of Life as it was interpreted by the Golden Dawn, well-known magic society of the period around the turn of the century. The Tree played an extremely important part in the organization of the Golden Dawn. In fact the progression of the initiate through the degrees of the Order was based on the progression of the soul up the pathways of the Tree to Kether.

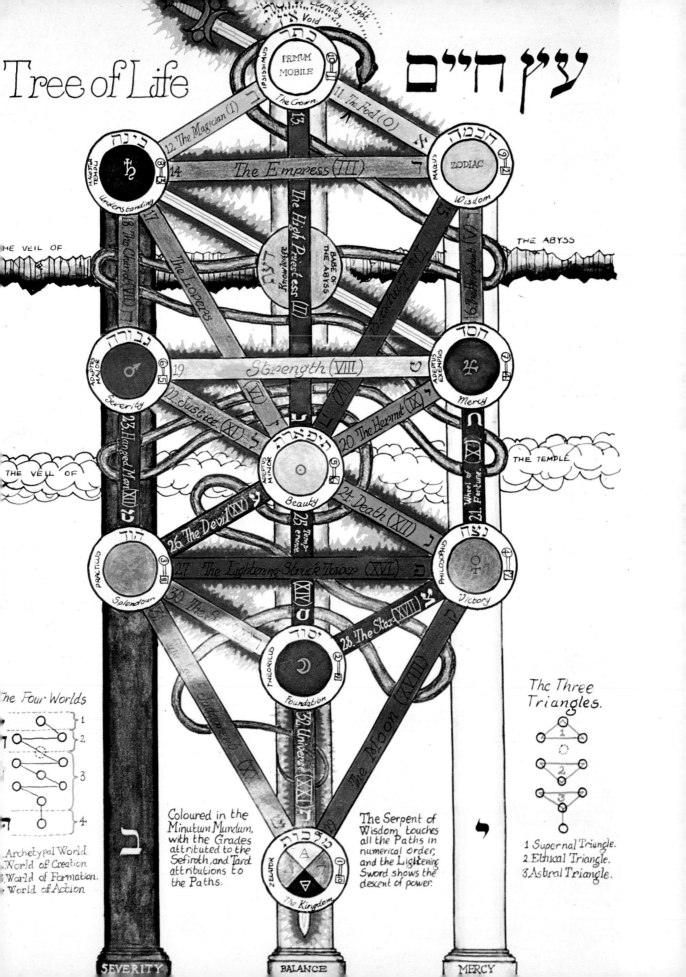

along the paths it is necessary . . . to hold the degrees of initiation to which they correspond; [for] unless one has received the grade, one will be unknown to the guardians of the paths, and they will be inimical rather than helpful, and do all in their power to turn the wanderer back.''

Assuming that he has the necessary degree of initiation and can satisfy the guardians, the magician now conjures up in the triangle outside his circle the required sefirothic form. He will probably make it materialize in the shape of the traditional image associated with the particular sefira. If he is working with the powers of Hesed, for example, the form will be a crowned king on a throne, and if with Netsah, it will be a beautiful naked woman. It is at this stage that the magician has to be prepared to contend with and banish the evil negative qlifahs. The sefirothic form cannot enter the circle, but the force it represents can through one of the archangels and the pentagrammatic gates. The force may even be visible as a swirling cloud of vapor. In order to build up the force even more, the magician also has to conjure up in the triangle the planetary form associated with his chosen sefira. When sufficient force has built up, he has to gather himself up for the climax of the operation.

The object is to draw into himself the elemental force that he requires to accomplish his purpose. To do this he must, in the words of Albertus Magnus, "fall into a great excess." He has to lose his reason and whip himself into a frenzy. It is at this stage that sex, drugs, alcohol, or bloody sacrifice may enter into the ritual, though they are not necessary. The frenzy may be by self-hypnosis, induced by chanting a word over and over again. Behind him, within the circle, the magician visualizes a god- or goddess-form materializing, growing, towering immensely above him. He must not turn and look at it for fear that it may be so hideous or so ravishing that the sight could prove fatal to him. Then comes the moment when the god- or goddess-form takes control of him, taking over and convulsing his body. At this same moment the magician visualizes the thing he wants to accomplish. He expels the accumulated force and bids it go to fulfill its mission. If his magic involves another person, an article of that person's clothing, a lock of hair, or some nail clippings may be used in order to put the magical force on target.

Having summoned up the magical forces, the magician now makes the return journey to Malkhuth. He goes back the same way as he came, politely thanking the guardians of the paths and sefiroth for their help and hospitality as he passes them. The archangels too have to be thanked. Finally the magician forms the cabalistic cross again to banish unwanted hangers-on—for minor psychic forces hover around a magical operation like moths around a candle, and he does not want his normal life disrupted by poltergeists, ghosts, or suchlike.

In 1963 the *Journal of Parapsychology* carried an article by the Czechoslovakian doctor Milan Ryzl entitled "The Focusing of ESP on Particular Targets." Dr. Ryzl reported on some telepathic experiments he had made in which a person tried to transmit intense sensations to another person miles away. When the sender concentrated on a sensation of suffocation and anxiety, the receiver suffered a choking fit. When he took a depressant

Above: Arthur Edward Waite, historian of magic, was fascinated by the Cabala. A member of the Golden Dawn, he translated Lévi's book on magical dogma and ritual. He also wrote a good many other massive and dense volumes on various aspects of the "secret tradition" which he claimed existed as a common element in Christianity, alchemy, the Cabala, Freemasonry, and the legend of the Holy Grail.

Right: Waite was absorbed with the relationship of the Tarot cards to the Cabala in which each card symbolized one of the 22 paths between the sefiroth. He designed a set, of which six are shown. It became one of the best-known versions of the Tarot.

THE MAGICIAN.

THE HANGED MAN.

THE FOOL.

JUDGEMENT.

THE MOON.

THE DEVIL.

drug and concentrated on feelings of despair and gloom, the receiver suffered from a prolonged headache and a feeling of nausea. The effects were clearly not produced by suggestion, for the receiver had no way of knowing what kind of sensations were being beamed at him. Dr. Ryzl's experiments caused some of his readers to adopt a more open-minded attitude than they had previously held on the effectiveness of magical rituals. If such strong effects could be produced under experimental laboratory conditions, how much greater might be the effect of the discharge of the intense emotions built up in the cabalistic ritual?

4

Magic Words and Spells

The Elizabethan astrologer John Dee had a most curious way of communicating with the spirit world. Before him on a writing table he would place a chart of over 100 squares, each with a letter in it. His assistant Edward Kelley would sit nearby at what they called the Holy Table, on which a similar chart of numbered squares lay before him. Kelley gazed into a crystal and concentrated until the figure of an angel appeared in it. Using a wand the angel pointed to a succession of squares on Kelley's chart. Kelley called these numbers out to Dee, who wrote down the corresponding letters. When the angel had finished, words of the message were rewritten backward.

The mysterious, unexplainable powers ascribed to magicians most often make them figures of fearsome drama, but in Gilbert and Sullivan's *The Sorcerer*, first performed in 1877, the magician was John Wellington Wells ("I'm a dealer in magic and spells"). He dispensed a love potion in a teapot, which put a spell on the whole town with most unexpected—and disconcerting—results. At the end, the spell is broken by the magician agreeing reluctantly to give up his life.

"To know the name...is to be able to tap its power"

The words were in a language that Dee called Enochian, and which he said had been dictated to him by the angels. The curious thing about Enochian is that it has grammar and syntax like established languages do, and it can be translated into other languages. Whether Enochian was the invention of the scholarly Dee or his inspired but scoundrelly medium Kelley, or whether it was really the language of the angels, its effectiveness in magical work has been attested by many practicing magicians. The language consists of apparently genuine words of Powers, and was used by Aleister Crowley in this invocation:

Eca, zodocare, Iad, goho,
Torzodu odo kikale qaa!
Zodocare od zodameranu!
Zodorje, lape zodiredo Ol
Noco Mada, das Iadapiel!
Ilas! Hoatahe Iaida!

The idea that words, names, and sounds have special powers is common to all magic. In numerology, the character and destiny of a person or thing is contained in the name. The same principle applies to the gods, angels, and demons. To know the name, and how to pronounce and use it, is to be able to tap its power.

The ancient belief in a secret name that had power over everything in the Universe was fairly widespread. For the Jews this secret name was the true name of God. In the Old Testament, God is referred to by various names such as Adonai or Elohim, and these are used in magic. But the personal name of God was considered so sacred that it was rarely pronounced aloud.

Right: design for a Great Seal by John Dee, Elizabethan investigator into magic. This drawing is from one of the notebooks in which he made a careful record of his magical experiences. The writing on the Seal is partly in Latin, and partly in Enochian, Dee's so-called language of the Angels.

Left: beginning of a manuscript that gives the magic ritual for invoking Venus. It is known to have been in Dee's possession and indicates that he had some involvement with conventional ritual magic. The following pages tell how to make the horn and circle, and summon the spirits. Throughout the ritual the color green—the color sacred to Venus—plays a very important role.

יהוה

Above: the Tetragrammation, the name of God, in its four Hebrew letters. Even in early times, it was pronounced only once a year. Tradition says that the sages were allowed to pass it on verbally to their disciples every seven years. That ancient pronunciation has been lost, and it is now, in normal Jewish religious reading, vocalized as Adonai, the Lord. **Below:** preparing a magic circle. Outside the circle is the first symbol of the Tetragrammation.

It was known as the Tetragrammation, or word of four letters. The four letters are Y H V H, which in Hebrew are yod, he, vau, he. The correct pronunciation is uncertain partly because there are no printed vowels in Hebrew, and partly because the word was spoken so rarely that there is no traditional pronunciation to follow. Scholars on the whole prefer to write and say it as Yahweh, although the English Bible renders it as Jehovah. Correct pronunciation is essential in magic, which may be why some magicians claim to be among the very few who know the secret.

More powerful even than the Tetragrammation was the Shemhamforash. It was the name of 72 syllables that Moses is said to have used to divide the waters of the Red Sea to enable the Israelites to escape the pursuing Egyptians. The true pronunciation of this name is unknown, and it is too cumbersome to be widely used in magic. But the number 72 has a mystic significance, and the Renaissance cabalist John Reuchlin ingeniously managed to link the Shemhamforash to the Tetragrammation by means of gematria, the cabalist method of assigning numerical values to letters. The numerical equivalents of Y H V H are: Y = 10, H = 5, V = 6, H = 5, totaling 26.

However, if the name is built up progressively and then totaled, it is found to equal 72, the same number as the syllables of the Shemhamforash.

$$
\begin{aligned}
Y &= 10 \\
YH &= 15 \\
YHV &= 21 \\
YHVH &= \underline{26} \\
&\quad\; \underline{72}
\end{aligned}
$$

This was the kind of exercise that delighted the cabalist, for the cabalistic mind avidly sought order in the mystery and multiplicity of the world. When cabalists found order they fancied that they had also found arcane knowledge. And in cabalistic thought knowledge was power. Knowledge of the names of the sefirothic guardians overcomes their resistance, and knowledge of the names of demons summoned up in ritual magic gives the magician power over them.

That it is not enough to know the words of power without knowing how to use them correctly is illustrated by a story told by the modern cabalist Israel Regardie. A young English student of the occult arts proposed to summon up an *undine*, a spirit associated with water. To make the invocation easier, he decided to perform his ritual beside the sea. He packed all

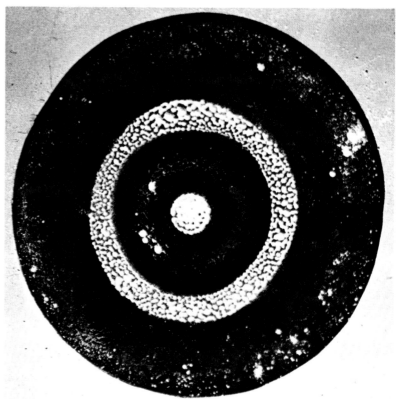

Above: Aleister Crowley, robed in one of the Golden Dawn ritual costumes, "vibrates" a magical name as part of a ritual for invoking a specific spirit. This kind of exercise demanded tremendous powers of concentration, and required a great deal of practice for success. Above right: a device invented by Dr. Hans Jenny to show sound visually revealed that the vowel O formed a perfect sphere shape.

his paraphernalia—robes, sword, gong, incense, candles, collapsible altar—and took a train to a respectable seaside resort. There, late one night at low tide, he went down to the sea's edge, set up his altar and lit the candles on it, drew out his magic circle and triangle in the sand, and began his conjurations, bellowing out the words of power in the still night. No undine responded. What the apprentice magician did succeed in conjuring up was "a wrathful creature clothed in blue—a policeman."

Israel Regardie explains how the names of power ought to be used. When the time comes for pronouncing the divine name in the ritual, the magician should inhale deeply, slowly, and forcefully, imagining that the God-name is being inhaled with the air. He should picture the name in the air in letters of fire and flame and, breathing deeply, he should draw it down into his lungs, then further down through his abdomen, thighs, and legs into his feet. His entire body should be filled with the fire of the divine name. Then, adopting one of the poses of the god Horus, as shown in the Egyptian Book of the Dead, the magician should exhale the breath that is now charged with the power of the name, imagine it surging up from his feet through his body, and pronouncing the name with "a mighty

Below: one of the central premises of magic operations—that sounds (magic words and spells) can have a physical effect—is verified by science. Here, in another of Dr. Jenny's experiments, a highly viscous liquid is vibrated at an ultrasonic frequency, producing a fascinating physical turbulence.

shout of triumph." If at this moment the magician feels his body full of force and energy, and if the name thunders through his entire being, he will succeed in magically vibrating the name. The effect of this vibration, Regardie matter-of-factly explains, "is to set up a strain in the upper astral light, in response to which the intelligence evoked hastens."

We know that at certain frequencies sound is destructive, that it can shatter glass and even kill a person. Magicians believe that the reverse is also true, that sound can be constructive and creative. Up to a point, science agrees. In an issue of the *Science Journal* in 1968 a Swiss physicist, Hans Jenny, wrote an article entitled *Visualizing Sound.* Jenny coined the term "cymatics" for the study of the effects of sound waves on matter. His work was a development of that of the 18th-century physicist Ernst Chladni, who discovered that sand scattered on a metal plate will arrange itself in beautiful patterns at certain sounds from a violin. Jenny extended his research to the human voice. He invented a machine that he called the "tono-scope," which converts sound to three-dimensional forms. He discovered that the sound of the letter O produces a perfect sphere—exactly the shape that we use for the sound in our script. Jenny's research has shown that sounds—and therefore also words and names—have properties and powers of their own. This is something that occultists and magicians have never doubted.

The ancient belief in the constructive power of sound is illustrated by the account of creation given in *Genesis.* The Universe was created by the *Word* of God. The divine intention or will was not enough in itself. It had to be expressed in the Word. The cabalistic belief in words of power ultimately derives from the *Genesis* creation myth. The power that God employed to create the Universe, the power of the Word, was believed to be a power that man too could acquire and use.

Among certain Buddhists and Hindus there arose a belief, similar to that of the cabalists, that there were words or sounds of power which, if repeated over and over again, could give man control over the spirit world. These were known as *mantras.* They consist of short verses with fairly clear meanings, cryptic words that needed deciphering to be comprehensible, or even single syllables. Some mantras were composed, some were the result of meditation or inspiration, and others represented the reduction of a large body of writing to a short formula. For example, thousands of verses of a holy book might be summarized in a single chapter. This would be further reduced to a few sentences, then to a single line and, finally, even to one syllable. This syllable would be extremely powerful since it would contain the essence of the whole writing. It was believed that the mastery of the mantra of this syllable would give an intuitive understanding of the complete holy book.

Mantras might be addressed to certain parts of the body where they would set up certain vibrations. This was considered particularly important in healing. It was thought that sound vibrations underlay the whole universe, and that by chanting an appropriate mantra, all problems could be solved.

The mantra could be used in all kinds of ways as a magical

In the story of creation in the Bible, God created the heavens and earth by the Word. "Darkness was upon the face of the deep" till God said, *Fiat lux*—"Let there be light." And there was light. Right: in an illustration for a book about the cosmos written by a 17th-century Englishman, the word of God takes an oddly serpentine form as it coils in an explosion of light, incorporating the dove which symbolizes the spirit of God.

Below: in one of Michelangelo's frescos for the Sistine Chapel in the Vatican, the Creation is expressed by gesture—which is more common to most than the concept of Creation by sound.

Right: the cabalistic seal of Cornelius Agrippa. It is made up of abbreviations formed by having each letter represent the first letter of another word, thus compressing and presumably heightening the power of the entire phrase. In this seal, the word is "Araita," which uses the initial letters of each of the Hebrew names of God. The principle is similar to that used to make up the mantras of the Buddhists and the Hindus.

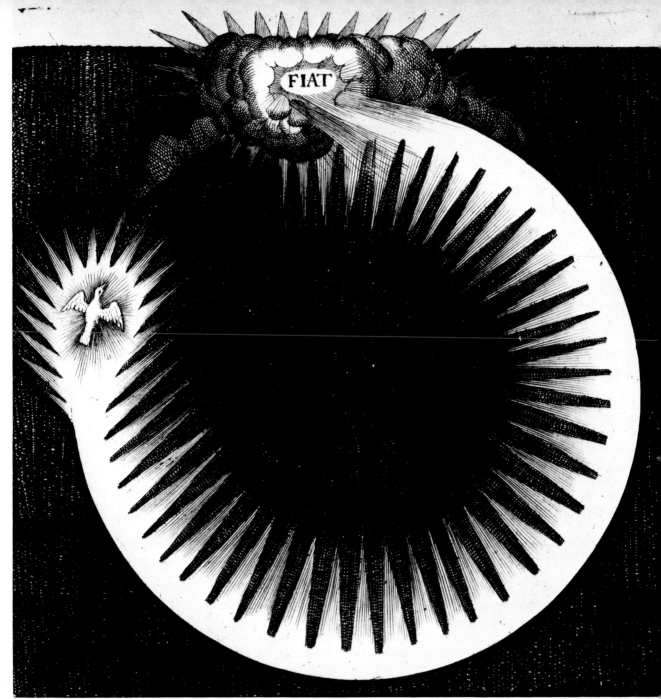

spell. Strings of dried seeds were often used to keep count of the number of times a mantra had been repeated. Sometimes, when the purpose of the mantra was evil, small bones of dead animals or humans were strung together and used in the same way. Extraordinary powers were associated with the repetition of certain mantras. It was said that if a special mantra were repeated 100,000 times, the chanter would get complete obedience from other humans. If it were repeated 200,000 times, the chanter would gain power over all natural phenomena, and if it were increased to a million and a half times, the chanter would be able to travel through the Universe.

Some of the most famous mantras are those using seed sounds, single syllables that usually end with an n or an m and therefore have an echoing, humming note. The best known of these is *Om*, which symbolizes all the sounds in the Universe. Its echoes are thought to encompass Heaven, Hell, and Earth, and it is supposed to be the key to the Universe.

In describing word magic thus far we have been concerned with the highest aspiration of the magician to contact and use divine or elemental forces. Magic at this level is the secret and cherished art of the few, the initiates, the priesthood. It is an expression of man's aspiration to be like a god. But in all countries, cultures, and ages, verbal magic has been practiced on a lower level—for personal gain or satisfaction, to insure success in love or war, to repel evil influences, to cure ailments, or to procure the fulfillment of any conceivable human wish or whim. Magic with such aims is appropriately called "low" magic. This generally combines some action, which may be simple or elaborate but is never as emotionally demanding as the action of ritual magic, with a verbal formula or spell.

Many ancient Greeks and Romans believed that the power of a spell was without limit. When in Homer's *Odyssey* Ulysses is wounded in the thigh, the bleeding is stopped by a magic spell. "The wound of Ulysses the blameless, the godlike, they bound up skillfully, and by incantations staunched the dark blood." Circe, the enchantress, could change men into beasts with her incantations. According to the Roman writer Pliny, the belief that the women of Thessaly could enchant the moon out of the sky was so strong that during an eclipse the people set up an incessant din with brass trumpets to prevent the moon from hearing the spells. Fire could be controlled, rivers made to change their course or flow backward, crops could be blighted or enticed from one field to another, men rendered impotent or women submissive—all by the power of incantation or the magic spell.

Spells are often associated with plants or herbs. It was believed that the reason the Thessalian witches wished to bring the moon down to earth was to concentrate its influence on the plants they used for magical purposes.

The most famous magical plant is the mandrake. The true mandrake, the *mandragora*, grows only in Mediterranean countries, but there are plants with similar characteristics and properties throughout the world. In the East it is the ginseng, in northern Europe white bryony, in America the may apple. All these plants have a root that seems to resemble a human figure. Throughout recorded history and all over the world, the mandrake has been prized for its medicinal or aphrodisiac properties, or as a talisman, and a mass of legend and superstition has gathered around it.

The most potent mandrakes were supposed to grow under gallows, and were believed to be produced from the semen involuntarily ejaculated by a hanged man. They were thought to be living creatures, and to unearth them was a hazardous business. The recommended way was to attach one end of a rope to the plant and the other end to the neck of a strong dog. Then pieces of meat were to be thrown just out of reach so that in struggling to get them, the dog would drag the mandrake out of the earth. When uprooted the mandrake would let out a

Right: the beautiful Circe, using her magical spells to change Ulysses and his men into snorting swine. The idea that such powerful spells could exist was common in Ancient Greece.

Below: magic practically forms the plot in Shakespeare's *Midsummer Night's Dream*, with many spells accidentally misfiring. However, the spell on the Fairy Queen to make her love the rustic with the ass' head was intentional mischief.

Mandra
gore.

Above: a 15th-century drawing from a medical treatise showing a mandrake plant being pulled up by a dog. In fact, the mandrake plant is not particularly unusual in having a forked root—even the humble parsnip often has that—but the root does contain an alkaloid that can be used as a narcotic drug. In ancient times it was used as a pain-killer and sleeping drug. It early developed a reputation as an aphrodisiac.

terrible cry that would kill any hearers. This meant that the dog was usually lost. The mandrake-seeker had to take the precaution of blocking his ears.

This is one of the more grisly and far-fetched of the mandrake legends. A pleasanter one is the Celtic spell known as Lover's Mandrake, a fairly elaborate procedure to win love.

When the lover has found his mandrake he must dig it up with great care before dawn at a time when the moon is waxing. As he digs he recites the words, "Blessed be this earth, this root, this night." He must take the mandrake root home, and trim and shape it with a knife until he gets as near as possible to a female figure. Then, holding it in his left hand and forming a pentagram or five-pointed figure over it with his right he must say, "I name you____." Of course he gives the name of the unsuspecting object of his passion. He next should bury it in his garden, and pour over it a mixture of water, milk, and a little of his own blood while chanting: "Blood and milk upon the grave/will make____evermore my slave." The plant remains buried until the night of the next new moon, when, an hour before sunrise, the lover must dig it up while reciting: "Moon above so palely shining/Bestow this night thy sacred blessing/On my prayer and ritual plea/To fill____'s heart with love for me."

The mandrake now has to be dried out, a process that can take weeks. In the course of the drying out it should be frequently passed through a certain kind of incense that attracts the influence of Venus. The drying process is also accompanied by a verbal spell saying: "This fruit is scorched by that same heat/Which warms my heart with every beat." When the little mandrake-figure is thoroughly dried out, the magician-lover takes a silver pin and thrusts it through its heart, concentrating his thought on the loved one as he does so. Finally, he leaves the mandrake on a window sill where it will be exposed to the moon at night.

The obvious drawback of this Celtic love spell is that it takes time, which some might feel would be more profitably spent wooing the lady with a more direct form of verbal sorcery. However, not all lovers are gifted with eloquence and some become tongue-tied with unrequited passion. For quicker results with less trouble the impatient lover may prefer to try an Indian love spell. One such is given by Idries Shah in his *Oriental Magic*, with the instruction that it should be recited over and over again while the moon is waxing.

"With the all-powerful arrow of Love do I pierce thy heart, O woman! Love, love that causes unease, that will overcome thee, love for me!

"That arrow, flying true and straight, will cause in thee burning desire. It has the point of my love, its shaft is my determination to possess thee!

"Yea, thy heart is pierced. The arrow has struck home. I have overcome by these arts thy reluctance, thou art changed! Come to me, submissive, without pride, as I have no pride, but only longing! Thy mother will be powerless to prevent thy coming, neither shall thy father be able to prevent thee! Thou are completely in my power.

Even in Roman times the mandrake could only be collected with special ceremony. Unless this was followed precisely, the plant would run away. Later, the root came to be considered one of the Devil's plants, bestowing infernal powers. The superstition that the root shrieked when dug up was probably linked with this idea. The mandrake's cry was fatal to anyone who heard it. One treatise warns all to beware of a changing wind carrying the deadly sound.

Extraction of the mandrake root is started by gently loosening the surrounding soil around the growing plant. Then a dog is fastened to the root and, enticed by a piece of meat, is induced to pull the mandrake from the ground. The mandrake's scream is fatal to the dog, but the protected collector can safely pick up the root, then fill in the hole with bread and coins to placate the earth. The root should be wrapped in the finest white silk cloth.

Love Crystals For Sale

Dieudonne Langston, mother of three and a housewife, lives in the English countryside. She is an antique dealer. On one of her trips to a stately home where an auction was being held, she found and purchased a book of herbal medicines, published in 1790. About that time she was asked to run a stall at the local church fair, and she decided to make up some pink love crystals from an old recipe she had found in her book. Following the directions meticulously, she made up 50 portions the size of an egg cup. She sold them cheaply, and the whole lot was bought up enthusiastically. That, thought Mrs. Langston, was that.

However, strangers began to appear at her door asking for the pink crystals, and customers from the fair came back for more. They claimed that their marriage beds were happier places because of them.

Now Dieudonne Langston sells her crystals by mail all over the world. To get the right atmosphere for concentration, she does her brewing alone in her kitchen in the middle of the night, stirring her secret ingredients into a mysterious pink brew as she chants the proper incantation. Once, she says, somebody walked in on her—and everything went wrong.

Above: a maiden consulting a witch, who is dropping herbs onto the fire to produce an image of the girl's beloved knight. Love spells are one form of magic which appear to have an endless popularity.

Right: in *Love's Enchantment*, a 17th-century Flemish painting, a young witch anoints herself with herbs such as henbane, belladonna, and hemlock to prepare herself for a magical experience of love.

"O Mitra, O Varuna, strip her of willpower! I, I alone, wield power over the heart and mind of my beloved!"

All that the lover-magician has to do in addition to reciting this spell repeatedly is to make an arrow, which represents the arrow of love, and wave it about as he speaks.

Other methods to gain a woman's love by means of a magic spell are given in the medieval black magic books known as *grimoires*. One is very simple, though it could possibly arouse the woman's laughter rather than her passion. While conversing with her alone, the would-be lover makes her look straight into his eyes and says in a compelling voice, "Kaphe, kasita, non Kapheta et publica filii omnibus suis." The book offers this advice and assurance: "Do not be suprised at or ashamed of these enigmatical words whose occult meaning you do not know; for if you pronounce them with sufficient faith you will very soon possess her love."

Love and lust are not always easily distinguishable, even by those concerned, but there are spells in the black books that seek to fulfill only erotic fantasies. According to the *Grimorium Verum*, it is a simple matter to make a girl dance in the nude against her will. All the man needs to do is to write the word *Frutimiere* on virgin parchment with the blood of a bat. The parchment is laid on a stone over which a Mass has been said, and then put under the threshold of a door the unsuspecting girl is sure to pass. It will compel her to enter that house or room, take off all her clothes, and dance wildly until the spell is removed. The book warns, however, that her "grimaces and contortions will cause more pity than desire," so this spell will appeal more to sadists than to lechers.

According to another grimoire, anyone can be made to dance wildly—though not in the nude—by putting under a threshold a parchment with the words SATOR AREPO TENET OPERA

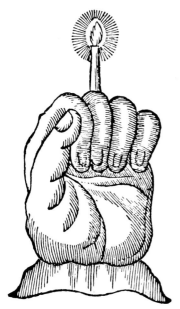

One particularly revolting charm is the Hand of Glory, made from a human hand cut from a hanged man, then dried and pickled. It was reputed to prevent sleepers from wakening, or to stupefy anyone who was awake—an obvious help to nocturnal robberies. Above: a 19th-century Hand of Glory used as a candle holder. Below: a dried Hand of Glory. The fingertips themselves are used as candles when set alight.

ROTAS written on it in bat's blood. Even your good old solemn minister will not be able to resist the power of this spell, the book says, and anyone who tries the trick will be assured of a good laugh.

Absurd though these spells are, they show that men's idea of entertainment has not changed much over the centuries—except that today they go to the cinema for erotic fantasies and slapstick comedy. It is another area in which the skills of the technologist have usurped those of the magician.

The written spell in the above example is of particular interest because it forms what is known as a magic square. *Palindromes* (words or phrases that read the same backward or foreward) are believed by magicians to have extraordinary power, and when they can be arranged in a square their power is all the greater. The Sator square is the most perfect because the words remain the same whichever way they are read:

S A T O R
A R E P O
T E N E T
O P E R A
R O T A S

In addition to making people dance against their will, this formula was believed to be useful for discovering witches because they could not stay in a room where it had been placed. It also gave protection against various ailments. This square was believed to have sinister power:

```
C A S E D
A Z O T E
B O R O S
E T O Z A
D E B A C
```

This one conferred the dubious privilege of being able to fly through the air in the form of a crow:

```
R O L O R
O B U F O
L U A U L
O F U B O
R O L O R
```

It is not essential for a magic square to have the characteristics of a palindrome. According to the *Kabbalistic Secrets of the Master Aptolcater, Mage of Adrianople, Handed Down from the Greatest Antiquity*, a book published in England in 1724, the following square can be used to cause discord:

```
H D H D H
I D I D I
D H D H D
D I D I D
```

Master Aptolcater's instructions for using this square state that it should be scratched with an iron point on a piece of lead, and worn in a leather pouch around the neck. When you start two people quarreling or fighting, you shout seven times to each quarter of the globe the words *Roudmo* and *Pharrua*, say their names and, under your breath, urge: "Fight, fight, Roudmo." The fight will be savage and unremitting, but the magician can stop it simply by saying the word *Omdor*. "In this way were many wars stopped in former times," Master Aptolcater assures us.

There are numerous spells that do not involve words or written symbols, but rather apply the basic magical principle of the system of correspondences.

Sage is a herb that receives the influences of Jupiter and Venus, and in magical tradition it has properties that the housewife who uses it in cooking would never suspect. The magician is advised to pick a quantity of sage at a time when the sun is passing through the sign of the Lion, grind it into a powder, and bury this powder in a pot in a dung heap for 30 days. At the end of this time it will have turned into worms. These worms should be burnt between two red-hot bricks, and made into a powder. This powder is very versatile. By sprinkling some of it on your feet you will insure that any favor you may

To Command an Unclean Spirit

In any invocation of spirits, particularly evil ones, it is crucial that the magician be of pure and devoted spirit. Otherwise the spirit will gain command over the magician who invokes it. According to an old grimoire, or book of spells, this is how to invoke unclean spirits:

Find a virgin black hen and seize it in its sleep so that it does not cackle. Go to the main road, find a crossroads, and on the stroke of midnight, make a circle with a cypress rod. Stand directly in the middle and tear the fowl in two, repeating "Euphas, Metahim, frugativi et appelavi." Turn to the East, kneel down, recite a prayer, finish with the name of God, and the unclean spirit will appear to you—dog-headed, ass-eared, and with the legs of a calf, dressed in a scarlet surcoat, a yellow vest, and green breeches. He will ask for your orders, which you will give as you please, and since he must obey you, you may become rich and happy on the spot.

As with all grimoires, the spell has been altered to fool the uninitiated. A magician will recognize the alteration. Someone else who tries it as it is will have "only his pains for his trouble."

ask of princes or powerful men will be granted. Put some under your tongue and everyone you kiss will love you. Mix a little with the oil of a lamp and everyone sitting in its light will imagine that the room is full of serpents.

Everyone would like to know how to double his money without much trouble, and the *Grimorium Verum* has a formula for this. Pluck a hair from near the vulva of a mare in heat saying "Drigne, Dragne, Dragne" as you do so. Buy an earthenware pot with a lid, fill it with water from a spring, put the hair in it, and hide it away for nine days. When you remove the lid, you will find a little snake that will rear up. When it does so, say, "I accept the pact." Put the snake in a box made of new pine and feed it daily with wheat husks. When you want gold or silver, put some coins in the box, and lie down for three or four hours. At the end of this time you will find that your money has been doubled. You should not try to obtain more than a hundred coins in this way at any one time, the book cautions. However, if the snake has a human face, as sometimes happens, you may get up to a thousand.

The black books of the sorcerers contain a number of unpleasant love spells (or perhaps, more appropriately, lechery spells). For example, to gain a woman's submission, take a dove's heart, a sparrow's liver, a swallow's womb, and a hare's kidney, dry them, and reduce them to a fine powder. Add an equal quantity of your own blood, leave the mixture to dry, and—difficult as it may seem—make the woman you desire eat it. She will then find you irresistible. The book does not say how she will rate your culinary skills.

If you want to make sure that your woman will not desire

A modern reconstruction of a complex medieval spell to preserve the chastity of a noble maiden while her betrothed is away at the wars. The magician begins by making a magic circle. Above: he then waves his censer, exactly as the ritual commands, over the circle he has prepared.

Right: the maiden enters, clothed only in a white veil. She carries in her left hand a rose, which symbolizes human love, and in her right hand a lily, which symbolizes human mortality.

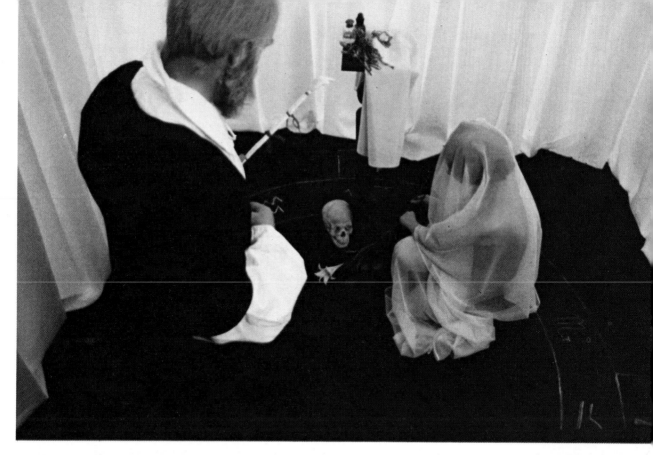

Above: directed by the magician, the girl lays her flowers in front of the skull within the circle as homage to the magical power that the ceremony is about to invoke for her protection.
Right: she places rosemary and verbena herbs next to her heart.

another man, take the genitals of a wolf and some hairs from his cheeks, eyebrows, and beard, burn and pulverize them, and give the potion to the woman in a drink.

To discover a woman's most intimate secrets, tear out the tongue of a live toad and place it on her heart while she is asleep. She will then talk in her sleep and answer all your questions truthfully.

The spell that is designed to subject one person's will to another's is the most ignoble of the magician's arts. It is far removed from the aspiration of the great magicians of the Renaissance and the ancient world to work in harmony with cosmic forces. Magic originates in our desire for power. This desire is not in itself ignoble, and it is often the origin of achievements in the arts and sciences. The fascination of the story of magic is that it sounds and charts the deeper waters of the human spirit, the dreams, hopes, and longings with which we aspire to transcend ordinariness, limitation, and death. We should not therefore be surprised to find in the story as it unfolds a mingling of the baser and the nobler aspects of human nature.

5

Number Magic

For all of us some numbers have special significance. Hotels often do not number the 13th floor, things seem to happen in threes, and the seventh son of a seventh son is somehow different—even if not, as tradition would have it, possessed of magical powers. Right: numbers and gambling have always gone together—on this early 20th-century postcard from Monte Carlo, Lady Luck poses.

In the 1880s Matthew Arnold, the famous English poet, attended a dinner party given in his honor by Sir John Millais, the equally well-known artist. There were 13 people seated around the table. One of the guests drew attention to this fact, and to the old superstition that the first person to leave a table at which 13 are seated would be dead within a year. Arnold laughed and suggested that, "to cheat the fates for once," he and two of the younger members of the party should rise and leave the table together. They did so. Within the year Arnold had died of a heart attack, one of the young men had committed suicide, and the other had been

Above: for the 16th-century philosopher-magician Cornelius Agrippa, numbers had a far more important and profound meaning. Using Pythagorean philosophies, Agrippa worked out complicated relationships between the proportions and harmony of man, as shown here, and the numbers which were associated with them.

"Belief in the occult significance of numbers is deep rooted and widespread"

drowned. The superstitious prediction of death had come to pass.

Of course, this could be chance. There must have been thousands of occasions on which 13 had been at table and the first to rise had survived the year. The idea that 13 is an unlucky number is sometimes thought to stem from the fact that there were 13 at the Last Supper. But in pre-Christian civilizations, as far apart as India and Italy, it had already been said to be a bad omen for 13 to sit down at the same table. Belief in the occult significance of numbers is deep rooted and widespread.

In the ancient world science and magic went hand in hand, but where science investigated nature, magic sought to control it. Science of necessity evolved concepts of number and measure, and in doing so, came across certain odd patterns and correspondences. Magic was quick to seize upon these and use them for its own ends.

The recurrence of the number seven must have been one of the first discoveries of investigations. The week of seven days, for example. Of the heavenly bodies, the moon has the most obvious influence on the rhythms of life on earth. Its cycle, which we call a lunar month, consists of four phases of seven days each. This is our week. Seven was considered to be the number governing the rhythms of life, and also the number of completeness. There were seven colors in the spectrum, and seven notes in the musical scale. In antiquity there were thought to be seven planets governing events on earth, and these could be linked not only to the days of

Right: Titian's *Last Supper*. **It has been suggested that the idea that it is unlucky to have 13 at table comes from the last meal of Christ and his 12 apostles, one of whom betrayed him.**

the week, the colors, and the musical notes, but also among many other correspondences to seven metals, seven vowels in the Greek alphabet, and seven features of the human head. Seven occurs frequently in the Bible, and it is the number most associated with mysterious magical powers.

It is alleged that Joshua used number magic to bring down the walls of Jericho. He marched his army around the city walls for seven days, accompanied by seven priests carrying seven trumpets. On the seventh day they circled Jericho seven times, shouted, and the walls fell down. Various explanations for this feat have been put forward. It could be held that Joshua actually succeeded in invoking the aid of cosmic forces. Another theory is that the final great shout of the Israelites produced sound waves of a frequency to set up vibrations in solid objects, rather like a soprano's high note can shatter glass. The belief favored by skeptics is that all the marching and ritual activity was merely a diversionary tactic designed to distract attention from some of the Israelites who were busy undermining the wall's supports.

Sound is energy. The training of former Japanese Samurai, or warriors, included instruction in producing the "kiai," a fighting cry. The sound of the kiai causes a sudden lowering of the blood pressure, and is said to produce partial paralysis in the hearer. Our language recognizes this kind of phenomenon in the description of a cry as "blood-chilling." Science has discovered that low frequency sound of 3 to 5 cycles per second can rapidly

Above: among the Tarot cards, too, the number 13 is unlucky—card 13 is the card of Death.

Scauhti vn vbi iche vidir iiij. Anglos idem̄ m̄pungtes malos a
m̄ 4 cus terre ne llaret i p iiij. ptes regni cor pdicaturo

kill human beings. The discovery of the relationship between
sound and numbers is generally credited to Pythagoras, the
Greek philosopher and mystic of the 6th century B.C. There is a
legend that Pythagoras once happened to pass a blacksmith's
shop and noticed that four anvils of different sizes produced four
distinct notes when they were struck. Investigating the phenomenon, he discovered that the weights of the anvils were in the
proportion 6, 8, 9 and 12. He suspended four weights of the same
proportions from a ceiling on strings, and found that he could
produce the same four notes as the anvils when he plucked the
strings.

A plucked string sounds a certain note. If the length of the
string is doubled, the new note will be the octave of the first. It
may have been Pythagoras who discovered that the octave could
be expressed numerically as a ratio of 2 to 1, and the other known
musical intervals as ratios of 3 to 2 and 4 to 3. The fact that only
the first four numbers were needed to express these ratios probably inspired the belief that the first four numbers were the basis
of all numbers. This was given added weight by the fact that the
first four numbers totalled 10 when added together and only the
numbers 1 to 10 were considered to have great significance.
Other numbers were thought merely to repeat 1 to 10 in different
combinations. It was also found that the first four numbers were
essential in the construction of solid objects. One stood for a
point, 2 a line, which is the distance between two points, 3 a
triangle, which added breadth to length, and 4 a pyramid, which
is the simplest of solid objects. These observations led Pythagoras

and his followers to conclude that number was the key to understanding the Universe. They evolved a complete philosophy that demonstrated order and pattern where there had been chaos.

A man who works in a power station will soon become unaware of the constant hum of the generators. Similarly, according to Pythagorean philosophy, human beings are unaware of the "music of the spheres." Pythagoras anticipated the Copernican theory of two thousand years later in conceiving the earth and the planets as globes revolving around a central luminary. On the principle that strings of different lengths sound different notes, the Pythagoreans believed that each of the planets sounds a different note depending on its distance from the center, and that the combination of the sounds forms a harmonious cosmic octave.

All magic is based on the idea that everything in the Universe is bound together in a great design. Number magic stems from the assumption that this design is numerical, and that it involves assigning different properties to the various numbers.

The Pythagoreans believed that the odd and even numbers formed pairs of opposites in the Universe. The odd numbers were assigned the male, active, creative characteristics, and the even numbers the female, passive, receptive qualities. This idea has remained the basis of numerology down to the present day. It is not quite the arbitrary division it seems. It is based on the way the ancients represented numbers by certain arrangements of dots. Shown in this way the odd numbers look like this:

The even ones look like this:

The Pythagoreans saw phallic significance in the odd numbers because they have "a generative middle part," and they saw female sexual characteristics in the even numbers because they have "a certain receptive opening and a space within."

Furthermore, when an even number is divided in two, there is nothing left over, but an odd number divided in two had a part remaining. The odd number is therefore regarded as stronger, or male. Another reason for regarding the odd numbers as dominant is that the addition of an odd and even number together always results in an odd number.

The Renaissance magician Cornelius Agrippa in his *Occult Philosophy* lists the characteristics of the numbers from 1 to 9 as they would appear in a Pythagorean scheme. This is as follows:

1 stands for purpose, action, ambition, aggression, leadership
2 stands for balance, passivity, receptivity
3 stands for versatility, gaiety, brilliance
4 stands for steadiness, endurance, dullness
5 stands for adventure, instability, sexuality

Right: Joshua and his army, and seven priests with seven trumpets, circled Jericho seven times, then shouted and blew, and the walls came tumbling down. This 15th-century miniature shows the dramatic collapse of the city walls.

Below: a Japanese Samurai, or warrior. In his arsenal of weapons was his voice, trained to produce a horrendous shout—the kiai—which had the physical effect of suddenly lowering the blood pressure in an opponent.

6 stands for dependability, harmony, domesticity
7 stands for mystery, knowledge, solitariness
8 stands for material success and worldly involvement
9 stands for great achievement, inspiration, spirituality

It will be seen immediately that the odd numbers have all the higher and more interesting characteristics. No doubt there was a certain amount of what is today called male chauvinism behind the allocation of characteristics to the numbers—both Pythagoras and Cornelius Agrippa lived in male-dominated societies—but to regard the system as a crude and primitive example of male wishful thinking would be to miss the point made earlier: that the characteristics of the numbers are derived from their *mathematical* properties. For example, 6 stands for harmony because it is a "perfect" number—that is, it equals the sum of its divisors $(1+2+3 = 6)$, and it is divisible both by an odd number and an even number (2 and 3), so harmoniously combining elements of each. Eight is the number of success and involvement because when halved its parts are equal (4 and 4), and when halved again they are still equal (2 and 2, 2 and 2). The other numbers, likewise, have mathematical properties corresponding to moral and psychological characteristics.

Cagliostro, the 18th-century adventurer and miracle healer who has been called "the last of the magicians," had all Paris at his feet in 1785 because of the wonders he worked. He came to Paris from Strasbourg where he was said to have carried out 15,000 cures in three years. He seemed able to win as much money as he liked at the Paris gaming tables. He also forecast the winning numbers in the lotteries three times for a certain Baroness, refusing to do so a fourth time on the grounds that he had already given her enough information to make three fortunes. Healing and gaming were not his only occult accomplishments. At a gathering in the home of a friend one day he demonstrated his skill as a numerologist. Analyzing the names of King Louis XVI and Queen Marie Antoinette, he made predictions about their fate. The king, he said, was "condemned to lose his head before his 39th year for being guilty of war." Marie Antoinette would be "unfortunate, unhappy in France, a queen without a throne or money, wrinkled prematurely through grief, kept on a meager diet, imprisoned, beheaded." These were to prove two of the most remarkably accurate predictions ever recorded.

Cagliostro employed a system of numerology passed down from Cornelius Agrippa and, in turn, based on the Hebrew alphabet. Although the cabalists developed numerology as a method of prediction, character reading, and divination, numbers were most important as the basis of cabalistic philosophy. The gematria was the part of the Cabala that dealt with the conversion of words into numerical values. It was believed that God had created the world by pronouncing the names of things, and that each of the 22 letters of the Hebrew alphabet were divine instruments of creation. Each letter was allocated to one of the 22 paths of the Tree of Life, and each letter had a numerical equivalent.

The cabalists believed that a name mystically encodes the essential character of a person or thing as well as information

PITHAGORAS PHILOSO PHE GREC

Above: Pythagoras, who believed that numbers were the key to the universe. A Greek philosopher active around 530 B.C., he is traditionally believed to have traveled widely, and certainly was familiar with ideas that originated in Asia Minor.

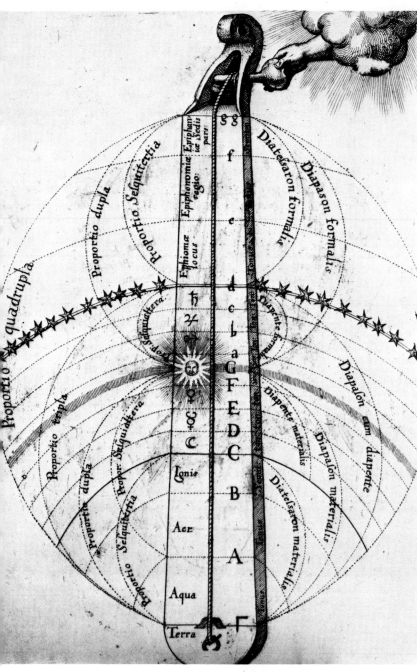

Left: the Music of the World, from Robert Fludd's book printed in 1617 and based on Pythagorean ideas. The universe is presented in terms of musical intervals along a great monochord that stretches from heaven to earth. Fludd was an English physician who was greatly influenced by John Dee and followed him in speculation and investigation of various metaphysical concepts. Below: four illustrations taken from a book published in Italy in 1492. They show Jubal, the biblical father of music, with Pythagoras and a student aide, experimenting with the tones of different musical instruments.

Below: the frontispiece to *Raphael's Witch* or *Oracle of The Future* published in England in 1831. It shows the Wheel of Pythagoras, a device used in one method of numerical fortune-telling. Among the decorative figures are a witch (in the center) and an astrologer, who is contemplating the heavens in the bottom left corner. By this time, the name of Pythagoras had become associated with almost any form of magical numerology.

about its destiny. The gematria was a method of reading a code by reducing names to number values, and discovering information about them through words of the same number value.

In the Book of Daniel, which was written in the second century B.C., the name Nebuchadnezzar was used to hide the identity of King Antiochus Epiphanes. It was carefully chosen so that the numbers of the letters in it added up to 423, just as did Antiochus Epiphanes. Cabalists believed that God, like the author of Daniel, used numbers in mysterious ways. For example, they believed that the three men who stood by Abraham on the plains of Mamre were the three senior archangels because the words in *Genesis*, "and lo three men stood by him," add up to the number 701, and this same number is obtained by adding

"RAPHAEL'S WITCH" OR "ORACLE OF THE FUTURE."

THE MYSTICAL WHEEL OF PYTHAGORAS

THE FIRST FIVE COLOURED DESIGNS BY RAPHAEL & R. CRUIKSHANK.

together the number equivalents of the letters in the words, "these are Michael, Gabriel, and Raphael."

Cabalists throughout the centuries have devoted years of their lives to proving the hidden meanings of the scriptures by the methods of gematria. No records exist of those who became mentally deranged in the process, but the most notorious cabalistic magician of modern times, Aleister Crowley, had a gematria mania. He identified himself with the Great Beast that comes out of the sea in the Book of Revelation and signed his letters To Mega Therion because the letters of these words add up to 666, the number of the Beast. The historian Macaulay would have disagreed with him, however. He thought the House of Commons was the Great Beast because the number of its members and permanent officials was 666 at that time.

The gematria provided a means of decoding material by converting letters to numbers. The Pythagoreans furnished a method of interpreting the numbers by the qualities they assigned to them. Judaism and Christianity contributed additional interpretations—and thus numerology was born.

The method of conversion that Cagliostro used gives numerical values to the letters of the alphabet as follows:

1	2	3	4	5	6	7	8
A	B	C	D	E	U	O	F
I	K	G	M	H	V	Z	P
Q	R	L	T	N	W		
J		S			X		
Y							

This system is based on correspondences between the Hebrew alphabet and ours, and there are no letters for the numerical value 9 because the Hebrew letters that stood for it have no equivalents in our alphabet.

An alternative method assigns the values by putting the alphabet in its normal order:

1	2	3	4	5	6	7	8	9
A	B	C	D	E	F	G	H	I
J	K	L	M	N	O	P	Q	R
S	T	U	V	W	X	Y	Z	

Below: ladies consulting the magician Cagliostro about the royal lottery of France. His brilliance in selecting winning numbers helped make him the darling of Paris society for a time, until he became entangled in the Affair of the Diamond Necklace of Marie Antoinette. Although innocent of the swindle, he was thoroughly disgraced. Cagliostro was one of the leading magicians of his day, but came to a miserable and unhappy end.

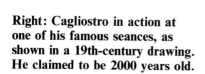

Right: Cagliostro in action at one of his famous seances, as shown in a 19th-century drawing. He claimed to be 2000 years old.

Different numerologists favor one system or the other, though on the whole the Hebrew system is preferred because of its antiquity. To determine the meaning of a name, and therefore the essential character of its owner, the name must first be reduced to one of the numbers below 10. To do this, the numerical values for each letter are added up, and then the individual numbers of that total are added together. If the new total is still more than 10, the individual numbers are again added. Eventually the total will be under 10. Here is an example using my own name.

S T U A R T   H O L R O Y D
3 4 6 1 2 4   5 7 3 2 7 1 4 = 49;
$$(4+9) = 13; (1+3) = 4$$

My "name number" comes out to be 4. Two further significant numbers may be obtained by adding the vowels and the consonants separately. Because vowels are not written in Hebrew, they are taken to signify the hidden self in numerology, whereas the consonants represent the outer personality. In my name it will be seen that the vowels total 21, which reduces to the number 3. The consonants total 28, which yields the "personality number" 1 $(2+8 = 10;$ and $1+0 = 1)$. My numerological character reading suggests that my essential character and destiny is a 4, my secret life is a 3, and my outward personality is a 1.

In the following key to the interpretation of the numbers, it will be seen that the basic characteristics ascribed by the Pythagoreans remain, but have been expanded and modified by Judaic-Christian thought and attitudes.

1: the number of God, the One, the Father, the Jehovah of the Old Testament. It signifies dominance, drive, leadership, singleness of mind and purpose, self-mastery, independence. People with the number one are powerful individuals, capable of great achievement, but also capable of obstinately following a path that leads to disaster. They set little store by friendship or cooperation, and are inclined to put themselves first.

2: the number of the eternal female. It signifies passivity, subordination, even temper, conciliatoriness, and desire for peace and balance. People with this number can be characterized by sound balanced judgment, generosity, and friendship. On the other hand, two also carries associations with the Devil, and a person of this number can be cruel, deceitful, and malicious. Two is a neutral number that can become good or evil by a combination of factors and its possessor is likely to be indecisive and susceptible to influence.

3: the number of creation and procreation representing both spiritual and sexual creative power. It is a powerful number, signifying the reconciliation of the opposites apparent in two. People with this number are talented, imaginative, gay, versatile, energetic, and often lucky. Its association with the Christian concept of the Holy Trinity endowed this number with a more profound, mystic, and spiritual significance than it had for the Pythagoreans.

4: endurance, firmness of purpose, accomplishment, will. It

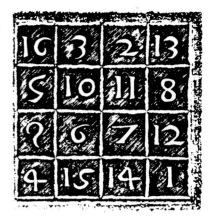

Above and right: *Melancholia,* an engraving by the medieval artist Albrecht Dürer, with an enlargement of the magic square shown in the picture. In a magic number square, each number from one to the highest present must appear only once, and the verticals, horizontals, and two long diagonals must all add up to the same total. Engraving the magic square on the appropriate metal at the appropriate time creates a powerful talisman. This particular square is the square of Jupiter, and each row adds up to 34. Thought to have healing properties, it was used to treat various diseases.

Left: for numerologists, Mark Twain is a particularly knotty problem. Born Samuel Langhorne Clemens, he was known at various times in his life as Samuel L. Clemens, Sam Clemens, and finally and most famously as Mark Twain. An analysis of his name involves tracing the development of his name number each time it was changed. He began life as a 4, with a plodding nature. When he went on the Mississippi as a river pilot, he shortened his name first to Samuel L. Clemens (name number 1) and then to plain Sam Clemens (name number 5). The number 5 would indicate his uncertainty and indecision at this period. But with the change to Mark Twain, his name number became 2, proving to be the perfect and stable balance.

Above: one favorite numerological exercise is to analyze the names of the famous to see if their known characteristics match up with the traits one would guess from their name numbers. George Washington's birth number was 1, and his name number was 7. This would indicate such attributes as his dominance and leadership, and his idealism and intuition. The frequency number 5, which occurs five times in Washington's name, indicates an adventurous vibration, offsetting uncertainty.

was a sacred number for the Pythagoreans representing completion, solidity, equilibrium, the earth. However, it is not a very inspiring number, and its possessor is likely to be rather down-to-earth, stolid, practical, and industrious. In its negative aspects it implies joylessness, dullness, and a tendency to gloom and melancholy.

5: sexuality pure and simple. It brings together the first feminine number of 2 and the first masculine number of 3. (One is considered the number of God and therefore not the first masculine number.) People with this number are likely to be adventurous, restless, quick-tempered, nervous, unstable. Number 5 is the natural man, the sensualist; but on a more profound level he is also the magician, the adept, the controller of the powers of nature.

6: the number of love, harmony, domesticity, union, fidelity, dependability, honesty. Having the power of 3 doubled, those with the number 6 can be very creative though on the whole they tend to lack the energy and flair of 3s. The negative aspects are conventionality, complacency, triviality, and fussiness over detail.

7: mysticism, solitariness, introversion, contemplativeness, aloofness, signifying the triumph of spirit over matter. There is a tradition that the seventh son of a seventh son will have

Above: Henry Ford in his first car, the "Quadricycle," made in 1896. He was 33 at the time. His birth number was 1, and his name number 5. He overcame the uncertainty associated with number 5, and with the purposefulness of number 1, made a fortune and built a worldwide car business.

magical powers. Seven is the characteristic number of poets, philosophers, scholars, highly intuitive and imaginative people. But 7s can be given to impractical dreaming, depression, and moodiness. They need success and recognition to fulfill themselves, or else they become frustrated and out of touch.

8: worldly involvement and success, drive, efficiency, capacity for concentrated effort. It is the number of struggle, tenacity, and materialism. Ruthlessness and obstinacy are the negative aspects of this number, and failures can be as spectacular as successes for those with it.

9: the pinnacle of mental and spiritual attainment. Passion, impulsiveness, broad sympathy and inventiveness are characteristics of people with this number. It is another powerful number, tripling the creative power of 3, and standing for completeness. It has the peculiar mathematical characteristic that when it is multiplied by any other number, the sum of the digits making up the final number is always 9. For example, $2 \times 9 = 18$ and $1 + 8 = 9$; $3 \times 9 = 27$ and $2 + 7 = 9$. This signifies a tendency toward egotism.

Another point to be considered by those wanting to try their hand at numerology is that the name used to arrive at their number should be the one by which they are most commonly known, even if it is a stage name or pen name. Any change of name in life is believed to be significant. Certain sects of medieval Jews nurtured on the Cabala believed that it was possible to overcome persistent ill health or bad fortune by a change of name. Few numerologists would go so far, but most would claim that the name a person is given at birth signifies his basic character and potentialities, and that any name later acquired or adopted yields what is known as his "number of development."

In addition to the separate vowel and consonant counts, numerologists pay attention to any "frequency" number—that is, a number which recurs several times in a name. It is also significant if a name lacks one or more numbers. In such a case the person is likely to lack the corresponding qualities of the missing numbers, and could therefore be unbalanced.

One English expert on numerology, Richard Cavendish, has analyzed a famous stage name as follows:

$$
\begin{array}{cccccc}
\text{M} & \text{A} & \text{R} & \text{I} & \text{L} & \text{Y} & \text{N} \\
4 & 1 & 2 & 1 & 3 & 1 & 5
\end{array}
\qquad
\begin{array}{cccccc}
\text{M} & \text{O} & \text{N} & \text{R} & \text{O} & \text{E} \\
4 & 7 & 5 & 2 & 7 & 5
\end{array}
$$

Name number: 2—the number of the eternal female (total count 47; $4 + 7 = 11$; $1 + 1 = 2$).

Vowel number (inner character): 3—signifying talent, gaiety, luck, versatility.

Consonant number (outer character): 8—signifying worldly success, power, wealth.

Frequency numbers: 1—drive, ambition, and 5—restlessness, instability, sexuality.

Missing numbers: 6—signifying domesticity, harmony, love.

The analysis would appear to be fairly consistent with what is known of the life and character of Marilyn Monroe.

Numerologists also take account of numbers in relation to time for purposes of character analysis, prophesy, and determination of auspicious and inauspicious days. A person's birth number—which is obtained by adding the day, month, and year of birth, and reducing the resulting number to a number below 10, as in name analysis—is believed to indicate the influences existing at the time of birth. Most numerologists stress that these influences get weaker as a person develops, and are modified by the characteristics inherent in the name.

The birth number is frequently used for the purpose of finding out a person's good or bad days. Everyone finds that some days are better than others, and that there are days when everything seems to go wrong and other days when everything goes right. Some numerologists believe that it is possible to predict such days by adding together the person's birth number, name number, and the number of the day itself, reducing the total to one of the numbers below 10. For example, my date of birth was 10/8/1933, (total 25 = 7) so my birth number is 7. The date today is 31/10/1974 (total 26 = 8), and my name number as we have seen is 4. Adding $7+8+4$ we get 19. Going on from that, $1+9 = 10$, and $1+0 = 1$, so the key number for me for today is 1, a number that stands for opportunity and action. The significance of the numbers in relation to the days corresponds with significances for personality analysis, as follows:

1 indicates a day for definite, direct action, for tackling problems; a day of opportunity

2 indicates a day for planning and for weighing problems, but not a good day for entering into commitments

3 indicates a day when many things can be done and achieved; a lucky day, and a good one for having fun

4 indicates a day for doing dull, routine things, for being practical

5 indicates a day for excitement and adventure; a good day for taking risks; a day to expect the unexpected

6 indicates a day for establishing harmony, reconciling conflicts, holding conferences, being sociable

7 indicates a day for meditation, study, research, for thinking things out

8 indicates a day for constructive effort, big undertakings, and financial dealings

9 indicates a day when ambitions might be fulfilled; a day of achievement, of personal fulfillment.

On the day of the Battle of Waterloo, one numerologist has pointed out, Napoleon's personal analysis would have indicated that it was a 6-day, a day for harmony and avoidance of conflict. For Wellington it was a 1-day, a day for decisive action.

Of course, many such examples of successful analyses can be put forward by numerologists to prove that theirs is a genuine psychic science and a key to occult knowledge. And anyone who tries it is likely to make some convincing hits. However, when we use numbers for fortune telling and for determining good and bad days in our personal lives, we have come a long way from the Pythagorean idea of the universe as a pattern of mathematical correspondences. It is also a far cry from the basic Cabala concept of numbers as the key to the secrets encoded in sacred texts on the nature, origins, purposes, and ultimate destiny of human life on earth.

Left: Napoleon. Had the great French leader consulted a numerologist about his chances at the Battle of Waterloo, he might well have been told that June 18, 1815 was not his day for winning. For him it was a 6-day—which is one for harmony rather than conflict.

Right: the Duke of Wellington, English military chief who defeated Napoleon at Waterloo. The big battle fell on a 1-day for him—a day for decisive actions.

Below: the Battle of Waterloo, which ended Napoleon's career.

6

Ritual Magic

A strange account of an act of ritual magic is given in the autobiography of the swashbuckling 16th-century artist-adventurer Benvenuto Cellini. The tale goes that Cellini, his 12-year-old apprentice Cenci, and two friends one night went to the empty Coliseum in Rome with a Sicilian priest who was also a sorcerer. Their purpose was to summon up demons. The sorcerer, clad in his wizard's robes, ceremonially drew his magic circles on the ground, and the whole group stepped inside the main one for protection. Cellini's friends, Romoli and Gaddi, were instructed to tend a fire and feed it with perfumes. Cellini himself was given a pentacle or

The possibility of a ritual that will summon spirits to the aid of the magician has proved a compelling idea for mankind all over the world. But similarly universal are the problems of dealing with the spirits when they do appear, and inducing them to leave when the ritual is done. Above and right: Mitsukuni, a Japanese sorceress, summons a spirit to frighten her enemies. It appears as a gigantic skeleton.

"Soon the magician began to get worried..."

magical five-sided symbol, and told to point it in whatever direction the sorcerer indicated. The little apprentice stood under it.

When the elaborate ceremonial preparations had been completed, the sorcerer began calling on a vast multitude of demons by name, in Hebrew, Greek, and Latin. Almost at once the amphitheater was filled with them. Cellini, encouraged to put a request to them, asked to be reunited with his Sicilian mistress, Angelica. "Do you hear what they have told you?" the sorcerer said. "Within the space of a month you will be where she is."

Soon the magician began to get worried because there were a thousand times more fiends than he had summoned, and they were dangerous. He asked Cellini to be brave and give him support while he tried to dismiss them as civilly and gently as possible, as was required by the ritual. Meanwhile young Cenci was cowering with terror, declaring that he saw a million fierce men menacing them, and four armed giants trying to force a way into the circle. The sorcerer, quaking with fear at this, tried all the soft words he could think of to persuade them to go. Cellini

Above: Benvenuto Cellini, the 16th-century Italian goldsmith-sculptor who had a terrifying experience with demons in Rome. The story comes from his autobiography, recording his often swashbuckling life in a surprisingly frank manner.

Right: a Japanese screen depicts the legendary hero Raiko lying sick and unaware of the horde of demons being set against him. His inattentive guards are no help.

did his best to encourage the others but Cenci, with his head between his knees, began to moan that they were doomed. Cellini tried to convince him that the demons were all under control, and assured him that he would only see smoke and shadows if he looked up. Cenci looked up—and then cried out in terror. He said that the whole Coliseum was on fire, and that the flames were coming toward them.

The sorcerer tried one last desperate remedy. He burned some asafetida, a stinking substance obtained from the root of a certain plant. This—and perhaps the petrified Gaddi's involuntary contribution to the foul smell—broke the spell. Soon Cenci reported that the demons had started to withdraw in fury. The group remained in the safety of the circle until dawn, however, and the magician meantime repeated ceremonial exorcisms. Even when they had packed up and were returning home, Cenci insisted that two of the fiends were still accompanying them, gamboling along the roofs and the road. The adventure had been a little more than anyone had bargained for.

Left: a miniature from a medieval account of a pilgrim's journey, showing his encounter with the messenger of Necromancy. The messenger, standing within his magic circle, shows the pilgrim how he can raise spirits. Around the circle are the suitable mystic symbols. The story tells of the various adventures the pilgrim falls into in his search for the true joy. Necromancy and his messenger are obviously one of the false joys the pilgrim sees.

Above: Eliphas Lévi (1810–1875). He was the son of a poor shoemaker in Paris. His real name was Alphonse Louis Constant, but he adopted the pseudonymn Eliphas Lévi when he began to write about magic and other occult subjects in the 1850s. The taken name was the Hebrew equivalent of his first two names.

Above: the magician Doctor Faustus, here in a 17th-century English drawing, stands within his protective circle and controls a demon that he has invoked. On the magic circle are written zodiacal signs.

Whatever may actually have happened at the Coliseum, it is clear that Cellini and his friends were convinced that they were surrounded by demons, and they were scared out of their wits. Today psychologists would be inclined to say that they were all hallucinating, the boy more vividly than the rest. This may be true, but the question then arises: what degree of reality do hallucinations have? The 19th-century poet Coleridge put the question another, more gripping, way. He asked: what if you had a dream in which you went to heaven, and there plucked a flower—and upon waking you found the flower in your hand?

Are the subjective and objective worlds as separate as we usually think? Neither the modern physicist nor the psychologist would claim that the world revealed to us by our normal senses is the whole of reality. Drawing on the insights gained into the physical world by relativity and quantum theory, the psychologist Lawrence Leshan has recently put forward the theory that two kinds of reality exist. He calls one Sensory Reality and the other Clairvoyant Reality. He suggests that both are equally real, and both complement each other and shade into each other like the colors of the spectrum. We conduct our normal lives at one end of the spectrum, that of Sensory Reality, but gifted mystics and poets move easily to the other end. Controlled laboratory experiments have shown that subjects under hallucinogenic drugs can also make the transition. Traditional ritual magic may be regarded as another technique for making this shift to levels of the mind where individuality can become merged in totality, and where the concepts of subjective and objective no longer apply. The powers of the mind at these levels are not fully understood, though science is beginning to take them seriously. It is not completely inconceivable that they might include the power of materialization, of plucking flowers from heaven, or of summoning fiends from hell.

Ritual magic is an elaborate and impressive use of ceremony carried out by magicians in order to conjure up spirits. The magician's aim is usually to gain some kind of knowledge from the evoked spirit, or to force the spirit to help.

Eliphas Lévi, the well-known 19th-century French writer on the occult, was perplexed by the problem of the reality of the phenomena produced in ritual magic. Although he wrote volumes on magic and taught the subject, he never actually practiced it much. But on one occasion circumstances so conspired that he could not resist the temptation to take a stab at it. His curious story was later used by the English writer Somerset Maugham as the basis for one of his short stories, "The Magician."

Lévi was staying in London at the time. One day he returned to his hotel and found an envelope addressed to him. It contained half a card cut diagonally, with the Seal of Solomon, a six-sided figure, drawn on it. A note with it read: "Tomorrow, at three o'clock, in front of Westminster Abbey, the second half of this card will be given to you." Of course he felt compelled to keep the mysterious assignation. He was met by a footman who ushered him into a carriage in which a veiled woman dressed in black showed him the other half of the card. She knew of Lévi through a friend, she said, and she wanted to offer him facilities for the practice of a ritual of spirit evocation. They drove to her

Let Apollonius Appear...

Eliphas Lévi, the 19th-century writer on theories of magic, seldom practiced what he wrote about. But when he was offered a complete magical chamber, he decided to try to evoke Apollonius of Tyana.

Lévi made his circle, kindled the ritual fires, and began reading the evocations of the ritual.

A ghostly figure appeared before the altar. Lévi found himself seized with a great chill. He placed his hand on the pentagram, the five-pointed symbol used to protect magicians against harm. He also pointed his sword at the figure, commanding it mentally to obey and not to alarm him. Something touched the hand holding the sword, and his arm became numb from the elbow down. Lévi realized that the figure objected to the sword, and he lowered it to the ground. At this, a great weakness came over him, and he fainted without having asked his questions.

After his swoon, however, he seemed to have the answers to his unasked questions. He had meant to ask one about the possibility of forgiveness and reconciliation between "two persons who occupied my thought." The answer was, "Dead."

It was his marriage that was dead. His wife, who had recently left him, never returned.

Above: the *Awful Invocation of a Spirit*, an illustration to a lurid romance, *The Necromancer*, published in England in 1825. It appeared in *The Astrologer of the 19th Century*, a collection of popularized pieces on magic and astrology. At this point in the narrative, the sorcerer, called "the sage," strikes the boundary of the magic circle with his wand to remind the spirit that she may approach no closer.

house where she showed him a complete magical cabinet and a collection of vestments, instruments, and rare books on magic. Lévi accepted her offer.

He decided to try to call up the spirit of one of the great legendary magicians of antiquity, Apollonius of Tyana. For this the prescribed ritual required a month of continued meditation on the dead person's life, work, and personality. The preparation also included a three-week vegetarian diet and a week of severe fasting. This was no small sacrifice for Lévi, who like most Frenchmen was fond of his food. But he suffered the ordeal, and the night chosen for the attempted evocation duly arrived.

Lévi tells how he prepared the ritual, uttered the prescribed invocations, and then—as smoke floated around the altar—felt the earth shake. A huge figure of a man appeared. But before Lévi could put the two questions he had wanted to ask of Apollonius, he fell into a dream-filled swoon. When he came to it seemed that the questions he had intended to ask were answered in his mind.

"Am I to conclude from all this that I really evoked, saw, and touched the great Apollonius of Tyana?" Lévi asks. He realizes that the circumstances he had created had put him in what psychologists today would call an "altered state of consciousness." "The effect of the preparations, the perfumes, the mirrors, the pentacles, is an actual drunkenness of the imagination, which

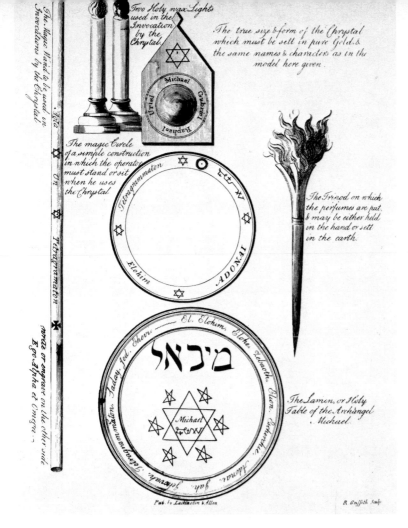

Two Holy wax Lights used in the Invocation by the Chrystal.

The true size & form of the Chrystal which must be sett in pure Gold, & the same names & characters as in the model here given.

Michael Gabriel Uriel Raphael

The Magic Wand to be used in Invocations by the Chrystal

Tetragrammaton

Tetragrammaton

write or engrave on the other side Ego Alpha et Omega

The magic Circle of a simple construction in which the operator must stand or sit when he uses the Chrystal.

Tetragrammaton

Elohim

ADONAI

מיכאל

El. Elohim. Elohe Zebaoth. Elion. Eserehie. Adonai. Jah. Tetragrammaton. Saday. Jod. Chem.

Michael

The Lamen, or Holy Table of the Archangel Michael.

The Tripod on which the perfumes are put, & may be either held in the hand or sett in the earth.

Pub. by Lackington & Allen.

R Griffith sculp.

Left: the equipment of the magician—the magic wand, the candles, the crystal, the tripod, the magic circle, and the "Laman, or Holy Table of the Archangel Michael." This illustration appeared in a handbook on magic by Francis Barrett, published in 1801.

must act powerfully upon a person otherwise nervous and impressionable," he writes. But he did not believe that the apparition had only been an insubstantial figment of his imagination. "I do not explain the physical laws by which I saw and touched; I affirm solely that I did see and I did touch, apart from dreaming, and this is sufficient to establish the real efficacy of magical ceremonies."

If this sounds incredible, consider some of the accounts of Tibetan ritual magic given by Alexandra David-Neel in her book *Magic and Mystery in Tibet*. Alexandra David-Neel was one of those extraordinary British women of the late 19th and early 20th century who traveled alone in the East in quest of adventure and knowledge. Her courage, intelligence, and fortitude led to her being honored as a lady lama. She was tough-minded and had a sharp eye for charlatanism, but she was not so conditioned by the Western way of thinking as to dismiss anything that didn't fit into its idea of reality. Living among one of the most mysterious and religious races in the world, she remained open-minded, observant, and ready to test for herself the rituals and disciplines by means of which the Tibetan lamas and magicians acquired and exercised their strange powers.

One of these powers was the ability to create a phantom being from their own mind. They called this phantom a *tulpa*. Despite a lama's warning that these "children of our mind" can get out of

their maker's control and become mischievous or even dangerous, Alexandra David-Neel decided to try the creation of a tulpa for herself. She took the precaution of choosing for her experiment a harmless character, a short fat monk "of an innocent and jolly type."

Preparations required her to shut herself away for several months, concentrating her thoughts and practicing certain prescribed rituals. At the end of this time she succeeded in creating the phantom monk. She came to regard him as a guest living in her apartment. She then decided to go on a journey on horseback, taking her servants, tents, and the phantom monk. In the course of the journey she would sometimes turn and see him performing "various actions of the kind that are natural to travelers, and that I had not commanded." On one occasion a herdsman brought a present of butter to her tent, saw the monk, and took him for a live lama.

Then, as Alexandra David-Neel had been warned, her creation began to escape her control. He grew leaner and his face developed a mocking, malignant look. She decided to get rid of the phantom, but it took her six months of hard struggle to do so. Reflecting on the experience afterward she said, "There is nothing strange in the fact that I may have created my own hallucination. The interesting point is that in these cases of materialization, others see the thought-forms that have been created."

According to Tibetan beliefs, it is not only human beings and animals that can be visualized and animated by mental energy, but also objects. Sorcerers are reputed to be able to animate a knife so that when a man picks it up, it can move, give a sudden impulse to his hand, and make him stab himself. The preparation for this act of murderous sorcery requires months of seclusion, concentration, and performance of rituals—including the calling up of demons to assist with the work—before the knife is considered to be charged with sufficient psychic energy to accomplish its purpose. Commenting on this phenomenon, Alexandra David-Neel suggests that the victim must have fallen under the influence of occult "waves" generated by the sorcerer. In other words, he falls victim to powerful forces of suggestion that annul his own will. It is a more plausible explanation than the knife itself becoming animated. However, it implies that ritual magic can be used to evolve mental powers which are, at present, outside our comprehension.

The talented and original 20th-century English artist Austin Spare not only evolved his own magical rituals, but also painted them and the materializations he evoked through them. Once he was pressed by two dabblers in the occult to demonstrate to them the materialization of an elemental.

Elementals are minor spirits of the lower astral regions, dedicated solely to representing certain elements. The main elementals are associated with the four elements of earth, air, fire, and water, which have been known through the ages. But there are hundreds more. These others are derived from the primitive belief that everything in Nature had a spirit—hills, trees, rocks, streams, and clouds, to name but a few. Like Nature, the elementals are unpredictable and changeable, more often cruel and hostile than kindly. Even more malignant are artificial ele-

Above: a self-portrait by the English magician-artist Austin Osman Spare, who died in 1956. His unconventional paintings express and illustrate his own system of magic, which he himself developed using elements of Cabalism and ritual traditions derived from the Golden Dawn.

Left: *This is my wish, to obtain the strength of a tiger* which records Spare's experience when he needed to lift an immensely heavy weight. To do so he magically summoned the strength of a tiger from his subconscious, so that he could command it. The operation worked; he reported that he felt a surge of great strength rush through him, and he easily moved the heavy weight.

113

Left: Lévi's interpretation of the Great Seal of Solomon, with which Solomon, in Jewish tradition, controlled the legions of demons. For Lévi the universe was entirely dualistic, with the polarities of light/dark, mind/matter, good/evil existing as absolutes and all manifestations a result of the interplay between these absolutely opposed qualities. Right: within Solomon's Seal are these elements, each carrying a particular significance. The triangles symbolize heaven and earth, meeting only at a tiny point. Man's role is to connect and balance them. The descending spiral is the creation of matter from spirit, the ascending spiral man's return path. Therefore the intersecting of all these symbols, as in the Seal of Solomon, shows man in a state of balance.

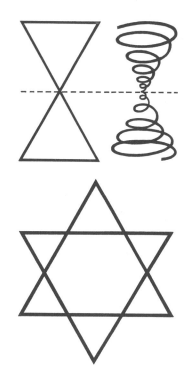

mentals, which can be created by magicians out of their own violent emotions such as hate, lust, and vengeance. Artificial elementals have only a short life span, but can usually accomplish much evil in the time given them. They appear as hideous animals or horrifying part humans.

Spare warned his friends that it might be dangerous to summon an elemental, but they insisted, and he allowed himself to be persuaded. His ritual preparations and evocations took some time, and at first it seemed that nothing was going to happen. Then a greenish vapor began to materialize in the room, to get thicker and thicker, and to concentrate itself gradually into a definite though amorphous shape. The phenomenon was accompanied by an overpowering stench, and the greenish mass became an immense face with two points of fire in it glowing like eyes. It filled the room. The terrified would-be occultists begged Spare to get rid of the thing, and he did so. Within weeks one of the dabblers was dead of no apparent cause, and the other had been committed to an asylum.

In his book *The Magical Revival*, Kenneth Grant, another modern magician, tells a story that sounds like an episode from a stereotyped horror-movie. It differs notably from Lévi's account of his evocation of Apollonius of Tyana, and from Alexandra David-Neel's creation of the jolly monk in that no prolonged ascetic discipline preceded the ritual. From Grant's story, it appears that an elemental may be fairly easily invoked, but not easily gotten rid of.

In the 1920s a group of magicians formed a lodge in north London. Its members were greatly annoyed when a rival lodge was established in the district, and they decided to punish the upstarts by plaguing them with the attentions of an invoked elemental. The newcomers got wind of the plot and performed a ritual designed to turn the malevolent force back on its creators.

Unfortunately for the original group, this ploy was successful. Their own elemental disrupted a cosy tea party, sent cups, plates, and sandwiches flying around the room, smashed ornaments and pictures. For weeks—day and night, at home and at work—all the members of the original group were tormented by the treacherous elemental, their own creation, which was said to look like a giant sea anemone with long spindly legs. They only got rid of it after several long ceremonies of exorcism.

Lévi said of ritual magic, "I regard the practice as destructive and dangerous." The foremost contemporary historian on the subject, A. E. Waite, makes it clear in the opening pages of his *Book of Ceremonial Magic* that he also deplores the practice as "the hunger and thirst of the soul seeking to satisfy its craving in the ashpits of uncleanness, greed, hatred, and malice." Waite calls the grimoires "little books of wicked and ultra-foolish secrets." He justifies the publication of his own *Complete Grimoire* only as a definitive act of scholarship and "a contribution of some value to certain side issues of historical research." The examples we have given seem to illustrate his objection to ritual magic as normally practiced for trivial or ignoble purposes. Yet even if all the "ultra-foolish secrets" of the grimoires are dismissed as charlatanism or superstition, and their elaborate

Below: a witch driving off evil spirits she has conjured up. Apparently she had raised the elementals to obtain the gold and jewels that are seen bulging out of her apron. Like magicians the world over, she faces the problem of dispersing the spirits.

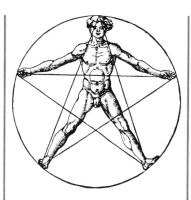

The Power of the Pentagram

The five-pointed star of magical ritual is a symbol both of good and evil. With one point upward, as above, it can be visualized as a man's body, and is a representation of the dominance of the divine spirit over the material world. Reversed, as below, the pentagram becomes the symbol of evil with the two upward points representing the horns of the Devil. It is used in the reverse position if there is a strong necessity for dealing with evil in a ritual.

The power of the pentagram comes mainly from its association with the number 5, which in number magic stands for the living world of Nature; the four directions and the center; the senses and union of the sexes; and man as microcosm.

Pentagrams are drawn in the rim of the magic circle to protect the magician, who usually wears the symbol embroidered on his or her ceremonial robes, or carries it in one hand as a further guard against hostile spirits.

rites as so much mumbo-jumbo, there remains a fascination about ritual magic. It is not merely the fascination of the outlandish and grotesque. It is our constant fascination with the strange powers and hidden potentials of our own minds.

Laboratory research by parapsychologists has clearly established the existence of psychic energy. It has been demonstrated that material objects can be moved in space by the power of thought. The Russian woman Nelya Mikhailova appears to have this power, called psychokinesis. Reports of laboratory experiments with her state that she takes from two to four hours to work up her powers, and that after a successful exercise in moving things by psychokinesis, she is exhausted and has lost weight. The Israeli psychic Uri Geller is said to be able to produce similar effects without such effort. He has also been studied under laboratory conditions. Many scientists have now become convinced that psychic energy exists, and are anxious to find out what it is and how it works. Some have pointed out that electricity, the energy on which the modern world is virtually dependent, has always existed as a hidden potential in the laws of nature. Yet we have only known how to harness it for about a century. From this, some scientists have suggested that psi energy might be as little understood and exploited as electricity was a hundred years ago.

A practitioner of ritual magic would say that he or she holds the secret the psychic researchers seek, and would find the analogy with electricity particularly apt. Before we could use electrical energy, we had to learn how to generate it, how to control and conduct it, and how to protect ourselves from it. Ritual magic claims to have this knowledge in respect of psychic energy. It is generated by the right ceremonies, and it is controlled and conducted by the techniques for binding spirits to do the operator's will. Magicians protect themselves from the danger inherent in forces they unleash by means of the magic circles and the ritual sword, pentacles, and so on.

The revival of interest in magic and the psychic sciences in recent years has contributed to the creation of a mental climate in which serious research into the supernatural powers of the mind can be conducted. It is difficult to imagine how a magic ritual could be monitored under laboratory conditions, but it is possible that something of value might be learned from the study of the ancient texts and methods. Alexandra David-Neel made the point in the introduction to her book on magic in Tibet, saying: "Psychic training, rationally and scientifically conducted, can lead to desirable results. That is why the information gained about such training—even when it is practiced empirically and based upon theories to which we cannot always give assent—constitutes useful documentary evidence worthy of our attention."

Anyone who studies the texts of the grimoires will be struck by the contrast between the grandeur and solemnity of the ritual itself and the triviality, preposterousness—and sometimes wickedness—of the ends it seeks to achieve. The grimoires are curious evidence of the coexistence in the human mind of sublime and mundane aspirations. But they are essentially documents based on a system of religious beliefs, and it is this aspect of them that is worthy of serious study.

Sunday	Monday	Tuesday	Wednesday	Thursday	Friday	Saturday
Michaēl	Gabriel	Camael	Raphaēl	Sachiel	Anaēl	Caffiel
☉	♌ ☽ ♋	♂ ♈ ♏	☿ ♊ ♍	♃ ♐ ♓	♀ ♉ ♎	♄ ♑ ♒
name of the 4th Heaven	name of the 1st Heaven	name of the 5th Heaven	name of the 2nd Heaven	name of the 6th Heaven	name of the 3rd Heaven	No Angels ruling above the 6th Heaven
Machen.	Shamain.	Machon.	Raquie.	Zebul.	Sagun.	

Above: Francis Barrett, the Englishman who wrote *The Magus*, subtitled *A Complete System of Occult Philosophy* and published in 1801. It was a magic textbook. **Left:** a table showing the days of the week with their governing angels and two pages from the Book of Spirits, from Barrett's *The Magus*. Each planet had its own angel, which the magician could invoke to attain mastery over the areas of life that that planet controlled. Barrett maintained he only practiced white magic, and the Book of Spirits shows an invocation to Cassiel, "chief of the spirits," urging him to "only swear in future by him who has created everything with one word and to whom all creatures are subject." **Below:** Astaroth, by Barrett.

Because magical power is not generated in normal conditions of life or states of consciousness, magicians operate on the assumption that it has an external source. Whether this is so, or whether it is really self-induced, is a question that we cannot answer. However, the various external frameworks that magicians use in their magic ritual enable them to give some kind of order and coherence to psychic forces. The cabalistic Tree of Life is one such framework and, on a far less profound level, the system of demonology found in the grimoires is another. But whereas magicians using the Tree of Life will seek to harmonize and tune in with the external forces, magicians using the demonology will aim to coerce certain spirits into performing certain well-defined tasks. The idea that spirits or demons can be called up and compelled to give assistance to magicians is believed to have its origin in various documents attributed to King Solomon. The first, the *Testament of Solomon*, is Solomon's own story of his acquisition of magical powers. The second, the *Key of Solomon*, is the original and most celebrated grimoire, allegedly written by Solomon himself based on his knowledge of magic.

The *Testament* tells a story about a young boy who was working on the construction of Solomon's temple. He fell victim to the attentions of a demon called Ornias, who robbed him of half his food and half his pay, and sucked blood from his thumb every night. The boy complained to Solomon, who prayed to be given power over the demon. The archangel Michael came down to Solomon and gave him a small ring with an engraved stone on it, telling him that with this gift from God, he would be able to bind all the demons of the world into his service. The king gave the ring to the boy, who with it captured Ornias the next time he appeared. Ornias was taken before Solomon, who sent him to command the presence of the chief of demons, Beelzeboal. Beelzeboal in turn was forced to bring before Solomon all the other demons. The king interrogated the demons as to their names, powers, and functions, and set them to work on the building of the great temple.

The engraving on the ring of Solomon was a pentacle, the five-sided mystic sign of power used by magicians for centuries. There is no mention of the magic circle in the *Testament of Solomon*, though it has been suggested that the ring itself was symbolical of the circle. In magic it is the circle that protects the magician during the ceremony, and he steps outside it at his peril. To the East of the circle he draws a triangle to confine any spirit that he might evoke.

In the *Key of Solomon* detailed instructions for the conduct of magical rituals are given. From it aspiring magicians may learn how they must prepare themselves for the ritual with a period of fasting, celibacy, and meditation; what they must wear and what symbols they must have embroidered on their robes, shoes and crown; how they should make and consecrate the pentacles; and how to draw the magic circle and inscribe it with words of power. The preparations are elaborate, but according to the *Key*, every detail is essential to the safe and successful conduct of an invocation.

There is great emphasis in the *Key of Solomon* on the spiritual preparation of the magician. By means of fasting, continence, and prayer, he puts himself firmly on the side of the angels before venturing to deal with the demons. The ritual itself is preceded by long prayers of a most solemn and exalted kind, consisting of profound adoration of the Almighty, abject confession of the magician's own sins, ignorance, and unworthiness, and a humble petition for God's help in pressing the demons into the service of the magician's will. After all this solemnity, it can be disappointing to think that the object of the ritual may turn out to be the finding of treasure, the persecution of an enemy, or the conquest of a woman.

Invested with power in God's name, the magician is able to command the presence of any of the demons. The *Lemegeton*, another work attributed to Solomon, gives a series of invocations for making a spirit appear, each one more eloquent and terrible in its threats of eternal damnation and fire than the one before. The desired demon is made to appear in the triangle drawn outside the magic circle in "invisible and pleasant form"—an important phrase in the conjuration because some demons can

Below: Astaroth, the medieval male incarnation of the goddess Astarte of the Phoenicians. He produces an infernal stench, but is willing to teach students about the great cosmic secrets.

Below: Abraxas, a fat-bellied demon whose name seems to have been the origin of the word "abracadabra," which was thought to be a spell of great power. His name adds up to exactly 365.

Left: the demon Belphegor, who was originally the Moabite deity called Baal-Peor, worshiped in the shape of a phallus. He was supposed to be very difficult to summon, although once there he distributed goods with great generosity if he liked the magician. One legend says that Belphegor came to earth to investigate rumors about the happiness and misery of married couples, and retreated to hell gratefully, happy that relationships between men and women didn't exist there.

Right: Behemoth, who according to Islamic tradition was placed by God under the earth to hold it firmly in place. The demon was probably derived from the Egyptian hippopotamus goddess Taueret. In medieval demonologies he is mainly described as a fat and rather stupid demon, with duties as a headwaiter in Hell. But his description in the Book of Job in the Bible is truly awe-inspiring—"He is the first of the words of God; let him who made him bring near his sword!"

assume terrible and monstrous forms. The magician then negotiates with the demon for the performance of the service that he was summoned for, and afterward dismisses him with due ceremony.

Because the powers and functions of the demons vary greatly, it is essential for magicians to know which one will best serve their purpose. They also need to know the demon's seal, which they inscribe within the circle. All this information is given in the *Lemegeton*, which catalogs 72 prominent demons, each of them a leader of legions of subordinates. Eighteen of them are classified as kings, 26 as dukes, and others as earls, presidents, princes, and marquises.

An idea of the variety of character and functions of the demons will best be conveyed by giving a few examples. Amon is a strong and powerful marquis who appears like a wolf with a serpent's head and vomiting flame. When so ordered he assumes a human shape, but with the teeth of a dog. He discerns past and future, procures love, and reconciles friends and foes. Buer is a great president who appears when the sun is in Sagittarius and teaches philosophy, logic, the virtues of herbs, etc. He heals all diseases and provides good familiars—that is, spirits meant to serve a single individual, usually a witch. Sytry: a great prince who appears with a leopard's head and the wings of a griffin, but assumes a beautiful human form at the magician's command. He provides sexual services.

Below: Asmodeus, a demon who belonged to the order of the Seraphim, the highest order of angels, before he fell. Asmodeus inspires men with such lust that they eagerly betray their wives. He plotted against those newly wed, and during the medieval period he was greatly dreaded.

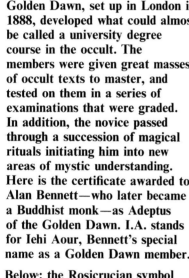

The Adeptus I.A. GHAB.A.M^c.G.

= Al Ayn ben Ayt = Ananda Metteya =

"Come in Peace - O beatified and divine One! - to a body glorified and perfected; Herald of the gods, knowing his speech among the living! Pass Thou through every region in Amenta until the place wherein the God dwelleth - because thou comest in Peace, provided with thy words."

Right: the Hermetic Order of the Golden Dawn, set up in London in 1888, developed what could almost be called a university degree course in the occult. The members were given great masses of occult texts to master, and tested on them in a series of examinations that were graded. In addition, the novice passed through a succession of magical rituals initiating him into new areas of mystic understanding. Here is the certificate awarded to Alan Bennett—who later became a Buddhist monk—as Adeptus of the Golden Dawn. I.A. stands for Iehi Aour, Bennett's special name as a Golden Dawn member.

Below: the Rosicrucian symbol of the Golden Dawn. Many of the Golden Dawn rituals developed from the rituals and literature of the Rosicrucian Society.

Glasyalabolas: a mighty president who comes in the form of a dog, but winged like a griffin. He teaches all arts and sciences instantaneously, incites to bloodshed, is the leader of all homicides, discerns past and future, and makes people invisible. Astaroth: a great and powerful duke who appears as a beautiful angel riding on a dragon and carrying a viper in his right hand. He must not be permitted to approach on account of his stinking breath, and the magician must defend his face with the magic ring. Astaroth answers truly concerning the past, present, and future, discovers all secrets, and gives great skill in the liberal sciences.

Shax: a great marquis who comes in the form of a wild dove speaking with a hoarse voice. He destroys the sight, hearing, and understanding of any man or woman at the will of the magician. He will transport anything, but must first be commanded into the triangle or else he will deceive the magician. He discovers all hidden things that are not in the keeping of wicked spirits, and provides good familiars.

Between them the 72 demons of the *Lemegeton* have the power to gratify just about every conceivable human desire or hope.

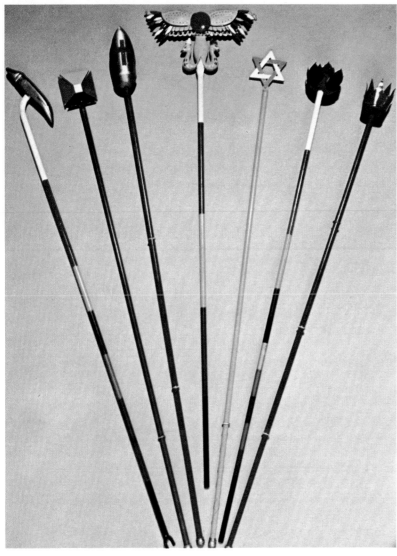

Left: Golden Dawn magical wands. When novices passed the rite of initiation for the grade of Adeptus Minor, their first major task was to make their own seven pieces of personal ritual equipment, using the color symbolism which was supposed to have been learned from the Secret Chiefs. In addition there were the wands, badges, and banners that belonged to the Order and were used in the initiation rituals and other ceremonies.

However, the book itself is probably more interesting as a literary curiosity than as a practical guide for the modern magician. Not only are its procedures extremely complicated, but also it demands too much by way of piety, credulity, and suspension of common sense to appeal to the modern mind. Apparently much more appealing for today's practitioner of supernatural arts is ritual sexual magic.

In Germany at the beginning of the present century, Karl Kellner, a high-grade member of the Freemasons, founded his own occult organization. He named it the Ordo Templis Orientalis, which became known as the OTO. In founding the organization, Kellner declared boldly that: "Our Order possesses the KEY which opens up all Masonic and Hermetic secrets, namely, the teaching of sexual magic, and this teaching explains, without exception, all the secrets of Freemasonry and all systems of religion."

The OTO had nine grades, the last three of which were concerned with the practice of sexual magic. Initiates of the ninth grade claimed that, by employing the appropriate sexual technique, any magical operation would be successfully concluded,

Above: Golden Dawn paraphernalia. Each detail of symbolism used on the ritual equipment was described in the Golden Dawn manuscripts, copied by hand to guarantee secrecy, and accepted as chosen by the Secret Chiefs. (They were invisible supermen who had given the original authority for the magical order to be founded.) The society eventually fell apart when more than one member claimed to be in contact with these mysterious Secret Chiefs.

Liber LXXVII

Oz:

"the law of
the strong:
this is our law
and the joy
of the world."

—AL. II. 21

"Do what thou wilt shall be the whole of the law."
—AL. I. 40.

"thou hast no right but to do thy will. Do that, and no other shall say nay."—*AL. I. 42-3.*

"Every man and every woman is a star."—*AL. I. 3.*

There is no god but man.

1. Man has the right to live by his own law—
   to live in the way that he wills to do:
   to work as he will:
   to play as he will:
   to rest as he will:
   to die when and how he will.

2. Man has the the right to eat what he will:
   to drink what he will:
   to dwell where he will:
   to move as he will on the face of the earth.

3. Man has the right to think what he will:
   to speak what he will:
   to write what he will:
   to draw, paint, carve, etch, mould, build as he will:
   to dress as he will.

4. Man has the right to love as he will:—
   "take your fill and will of love as ye will,
   when, where, and with whom ye will.' —*AL. I. 51.*

5. Man has the right to kill those who would thwart these rights.
   "the slaves shall serve."—*AL. II. 58.*

"Love is the law, love under will."—*AL. I. 57.*

Above: Aleister Crowley's brief summary of the doctrines of Thelema, which was to supersede Christianity as the gospel of the coming Aeon of Horus. It is taken from the Book of the Law, which Crowley said was dictated to him by the spirit Aiwass on three consecutive days in April 1904 when he was in Egypt. This postcard summary appeared in 1943, long after Crowley had been expelled from Italy to close the Abbey of Thelema, which he had established in Cefalu, Sicily.

from the invocation of a god to the acquisition of a great treasure. The techniques were, in fact, similar to and probably derived from Tantra, the Indian sect that uses ritual sexual intercourse both as a means of heightening consciousness and a way of worship.

Aleister Crowley was a lifelong devotee of the methods of sexual magic, and he engaged in autosexual, homosexual, and heterosexual ritual practices with equal enthusiasm. In 1912 he published material that enraged the leaders of the OTO, who accused him of betraying the secrets of their ninth grade. Crowley replied that since he was not a member of their ninth grade, he was in no position to know their secrets, and what he had published was entirely his own work. They saw his point, marveled at his work, and promptly appointed him leader of a British subsidiary of the OTO with the splendid title of "King of Ireland, Iona, and all the Britains within the sanctuary of the Gnosis."

The fundamental idea behind ritual sexual magic is that at the moment of orgasm a tremendous psychic force is released which can be directed to accomplish any magical purpose. The practice demands the same training in visualization that is involved in rituals based on the Cabala or the grimoires. The participants must be able to prolong intercourse and defer orgasm at will until a subjective reality of such intensity has been built up that at the moment of orgasm it is projected as an objective reality and produces a magical effect in the real world. Alcohol or drugs may be used to assist the process and, if the invocation of a demon or a planetary spirit is intended, the appropriate defensive symbols, incenses, and other essentials to the ritual are usually employed as well.

In *The Magical Revival* Kenneth Grant tells the inside story of the influence of Crowley on American disciples. It is a harrowing story of a series of personal tragedies, and it shows that the dangers traditionally involved in ritual magic are by no means minimized for those who choose the sexual practice. Few stories are more tragic than that of Jack Parsons, a brilliant scientist who became leader of the Agape Lodge, the successor of the OTO in California.

Parsons adopted the magical name of Belarion and named his partner, who was his second wife, Babalon (the Scarlet Woman). In the course of ritual sexual intercourse with her, Parsons contacted an Intelligence which gave him what he claimed was the missing conclusion of Crowley's *The Life of the Law*. He called his work the *Book of Babalon*. His life became obsessive, and his writings wild and paranoid. Crowley himself, dying in obscurity in England, was moved to reply to one of his letters: "I thought I had a most morbid imagination, as good as any man's, but it seems I have not. I cannot form the slightest idea of what you can possibly mean." To another disciple in California Crowley wrote: "Apparently he [Parsons] is producing a Moonchild. I get fairly frantic when I contemplate the idiocy of these louts." Parsons nonetheless remained loyal to Crowley and his doctrines, and declared, "In His Law I shall conquer the world."

He didn't. In 1952 while working in his laboratory, Parsons dropped a phial of fulminate of mercury, and was instantly

enveloped in a sheet of flame. Shortly before his death he had written, or transcribed from his spirit Intelligence, the following passage in the *Book of Babalon*:

"She is flame of life; power of darkness; she destroys with a glance; she may take the soul. She feeds upon the death of men. Concentrate all forces and being in Our Lady Babalon. Light a single light on Her altar, saying Flame is our Lady; flame is Her hair. I am flame."

These were prophetic words. Who would not rather undergo Cellini's harrowing night in the Coliseum than suffer Jack Parson's eclipse in derangement, paranoia, and flame? Both men's experiences may be read as warnings of the consequences of ritual magic gone wrong.

7

Prehistoric monuments—like
Stonehenge, shown here—present
a continuing challenge to modern
man. They were obviously built
for some specific purpose, but
the last man to understand died
centuries ago and the secret is
lost. What could it have been?

Books
in Stone

There is a legend that, shortly after the
crucifixion, the apostle St. Philip sent 12
missionaries to England. Among them was
Joseph of Arimathea, who had been responsible for the burial of Christ. In the West of
England, in an area of peat bog and winding
water courses, these missionaries were granted some land. In what later became known
as Glastonbury, they built a simple church of
timber and wattles, supposedly the first
Christian church built in Britain. It was
dedicated to the Virgin Mary.

Glastonbury became steeped in sanctity,
and its church came to be considered a holy
site. Lying as it does in the midst of the

"In the floor of the Mary Chapel was the Zodiac"

region of Arthurian legend, Glastonbury also had its share of myth. It was believed, for example, that Joseph of Arimathea had brought the Holy Grail to Glastonbury, and that King Arthur was buried in the church grounds. In the 8th century an abbey was built, slightly to the east of the old church, and later joined to it. When the church and abbey burned down in 1184, King Henry II ordered that both should be rebuilt. A new Chapel of St. Mary was constructed of exactly the dimensions of the original Church. The abbey flourished for many centuries, but had begun to decay by the mid-16th century. Its stones were removed for other buildings and it quickly became a ruin, as it is today. But growing there still is a flowering thorn bush said to be a cutting from the original thorn bush which sprang up when the holy Joseph of Arimathea stuck his staff in the ground.

In 1921 Frederick Bligh Bond, the architect in charge of maintaining the Glastonbury abbey ruins, published a remarkable account of a communication he had received through a medium. The message was alleged to have come from a monk who had been a member of the Glastonbury community in the 15th century. Part of it went as follows: "That which the brethren of old handed down to us, we followed, ever building on their plann. As we have said, our Abbey was a message in ye stones. In ye foundations and ye distances be a mystery—the mystery of our Faith, which ye have forgotten and we also in ye latter days."

Bligh Bond believed that in the measurements and proportions of what is possibly Britain's most sacred site, he had discovered evidence of the survival of a religion and a mystery more ancient than Christianity. However, whether his spirit communication was genuine or not, Bligh Bond paid dearly for publishing it. He was abruptly dismissed from his post, and the archeological investigations he had initiated were halted. The Church authorities in reaching their decision may have been influenced by the fact that Bligh Bond was not only a dabbler in Spiritualism, but also an expert on the Cabala and gematria.

The 12th-century monk and historian William of Malmesbury lived in Glastonbury before the original church had burned down. He wrote of it: "This church, then, is certainly the oldest I know in England . . . in the pavement may be seen on every side stones designedly inlaid with triangles and squares, and figured with lead, under which, if I believe some sacred enigma to be contained, I do no injustice to religion." This design was later completely erased, and no record left of it. However, according to Bligh Bond's spirit monk, "All the measures were marked plain on the slabs in Mary's Chapel, and you have destroyed them . . . In the floor of the Mary Chapel was the Zodiac, that all might see and understand the mystery".

A zodiac design might well have been incorporated in the mosaic pavement of the old church, but whether or not it was, the zodiac was linked to Glastonbury in a peculiar way. This link was discovered by the extraordinary Elizabethan scholar-magician Dr. John Dee on a visit to the Glastonbury area in about 1580. He noticed the unusual arrangement of the pre-

Above: the 14th-century Great Seal of Glastonbury, showing the Holy Thorn that sprang from a saint's staff. The thorn blooms just after Christmas. The original thorn was cut down by Puritans, but its descendents still flourish.

historic earthworks in the district, and was curious enough about the phenomenon to make his own map. The intuition that had prompted him to do so was proved correct: he discovered that the earthworks and natural features of the landscape were laid out in a pattern that corresponded with the zodiac. He wrote: "This is astrology and astronomy carefully and exactly married and measured in a scientific reconstruction of the heavens which shows that the ancients understood all which today the learned know to be facts."

Dr. Dee's discovery was forgotten, however, and was only exhumed from the mass of his papers after Glastonbury Zodiac had been rediscovered in 1920 by Mrs. K. E. Maltwood. Mrs. Maltwood, an occultist, was well acquainted with all the legends about Glastonbury and the surrounding countryside, including the belief that Christianity and the Holy Grail had been brought here by Joseph of Arimathea, and the tradition that King Arthur had held his court at nearby Camelot, and was not dead but sleeping forever in the hills. Standing on one of these hills one summer afternoon, Mrs. Maltwood saw in a flash the mystic landscape, the figures of giants sleeping, and the twelve signs of the zodiac. Each sign was in order beneath its appropriate constellation, and was formed by natural features of the landscape plus artificial banks, paths, and ditches. Aerial photography later confirmed Mrs. Maltwood's discovery, and scholars subsequently dug up Dr. Dee's anticipation of it. It would seem that the "sacred enigma" of Glastonbury mentioned by William of Malmesbury has something to do with the zodiac

Above: Glastonbury Tor, a hill rising to 500 feet above sea level, dominates the surrounding countryside. The nearby abbey is thought to be the oldest Christian establishment in Britain, and its traditions go back, with no break in continuity, to King Arthur, to the Romans, and even to the apostolic period. There is also a tradition that it was a pagan holy place before Joseph of Arimathea and his companions arrived and built the Old Church chapel of wattle.

Left: Glastonbury Tor from the air. At the time of the legendary establishment of the abbey, it was virtually an island, circled by lagoons and rivers. It was only when the abbey carried out massive drainage during its period of greatest wealth and power in the Middle Ages that the region ceased to be subject to considerable flooding. Even then, fair-sized lakes remained.

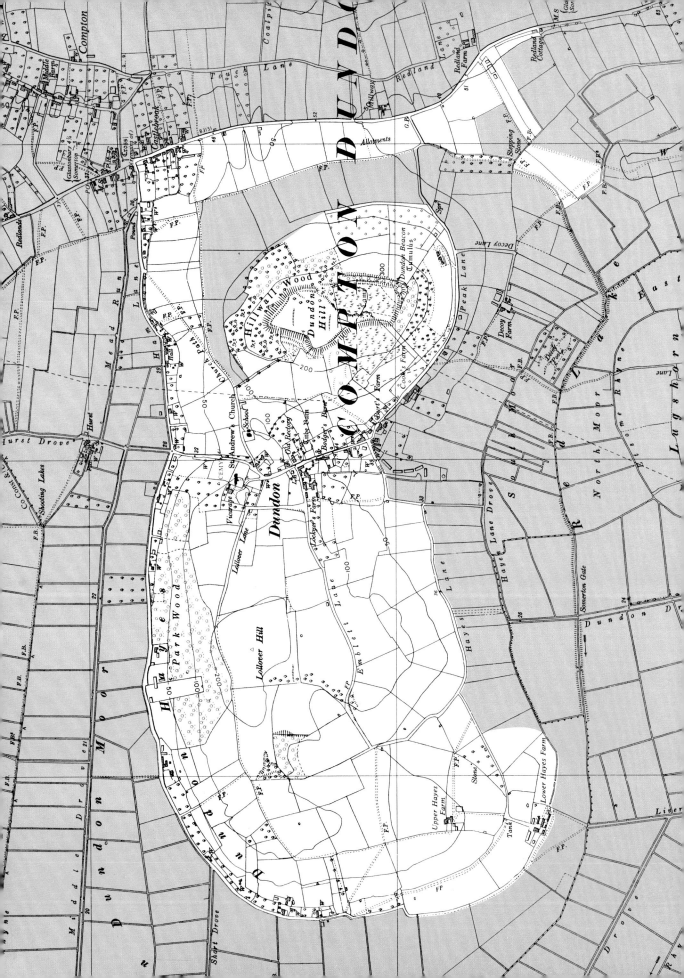

and the correlation of the heavens and the earth. To establish this fact is only to arrive at a further puzzle, however. Why should the ancients have gone to such trouble to mirror the patterns of the heavens in the features of the earth?

In 1967 a retired Scottish engineer, Professor Alec Thom, published a book called *Megalithic Sites in Britain*. It was the product of many years of independent work surveying most of the stone circles in the British Isles. His patient work was rewarded by two remarkable discoveries, both indicating that the people who constructed these stone circles were more than competent geometricians and astronomers.

Professor Thom's breakthrough came with his discovery of the principle unit of measurement of antiquity, which he called the megalithic yard (MY), and which is equivalent to 2.72 feet. Subsequent studies have shown that this unit of measurement is to be found in the proportions of ancient buildings all over the world. Applying this unit to the British stone circles, Thom discovered that lines drawn joining the seemingly randomly placed stones form precise Pythagorean triangles. From these triangles, circles and ellipses can be constructed, the perimeters and diameters of which can be expressed in multiples of the megalithic yard.

That the ancient Britons applied Pythagorean principles long before Pythagoras was born was a remarkable discovery, but even more so was Professor Thom's second conclusion. He found that the stones not only formed geometric patterns within and immediately around the circle, but that they also defined patterns in relation to features in the surrounding landscape with which they were aligned—and beyond that, in relation to the position occupied by the sun, the moon, or a prominent star on the horizon at a particular time. A stone placed outside a circle would be in exact alignment both with a geometrically fixed point within it and some feature on the skyline marking the spot where the sun appeared or disappeared at the equinox or one of the solstices, or the spot where the moon occupied one of the extreme positions in its cycle. Sometimes these features on the skyline were natural ones, like a hill or mountain peak. Where a natural feature was lacking, however, there would be a man-made one—a mound, a pile of stones, or a notch cut into a ridge. So consistent are these characteristics in so many of the remaining stone circles of Britain, it would not seem unreasonable to assume that at one time the whole land was constructed in terms of a symmetry bearing a direct relation to the patterns described by the heavenly bodies in their seasonal cycles.

So the Glastonbury Zodiac was not unique as a pointer to the prehistoric existence of a precise observational science of the heavens, a science presumably linked up with a belief in its relevance for life on earth. But what was that relevance? At the moment we know very little about what life was like when the Glastonbury Zodiac was conceived. All we can say is it seems most unlikely that a people who possessed such a refined observational science, such sophisticated mathematical and geometrical expertise, and such engineering genius, were at the same time ignorant and superstitious barbarians, as the ancient

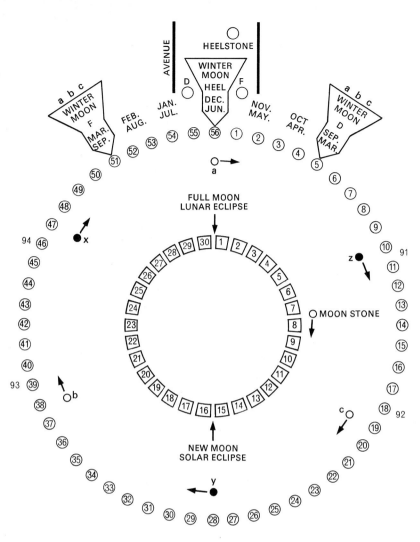

Labels in the schematic diagram:

HEELSTONE

AVENUE

WINTER MOON HEEL DEC. JUN.

D   F

WINTER MOON F MAR. SEP.

a b c

WINTER MOON D SEP. MAR.

a b c

FEB. AUG.   JAN. JUL.   NOV. MAY.   OCT APR.

FULL MOON LUNAR ECLIPSE

MOON STONE

NEW MOON SOLAR ECLIPSE

Left: Stonehenge as a computer—schematic plan by Gerald Hawkins. According to Hawkins, one method for operating the computer is to place three white stones (a, b, c) in holes numbered 56, 38, and 19; place three black stones (x, y, z) in holes 47, 28, and 10; and then move each stone one place around the circle each year. He suggests this be done at the winter or summer solstice. He points out that this will then predict every important lunar event for hundreds of years. For example, when any stone is at hole 56, the full moon will rise over the heel stone at the winter solstice. It can also be used to predict eclipses of the sun or the moon.

inhabitants of Britain are popularly believed to have been.

Let us look more closely at Stonehenge, the huge stone monument in southern England, through the eyes of Gerald Hawkins, Professor of Astronomy at Boston University. In 1966 Hawkins published a book entitled *Stonehenge Decoded*. The title was perhaps ahead of itself, but Hawkins significantly contributed to our knowledge of Stonehenge. His findings corroborate those independently arrived at by Professor Thom and published in the following year.

Professor Hawkins' discoveries had an extra element of glamour and prestige in that they were obtained with the help of one of the marvels of modern technology, an IBM computer. The Stonehenge complex has 165 significant features consisting of stones, holes, and artificial mounds. From these features 27,060 possible alignments can be formed. The task programmed into the computer by Hawkins and his assistants was to determine whether lines extended through significant Stonehenge alignments into space would coincide with significant positions of the heavenly bodies. Due allowance was made for the slight difference between what those positions are today and what they would have been in about 1500 B.C. The results were astonishing. Among the figures that the machine produced

130

were some that occurred frequently. These were found to correspond to a fraction of a degree in accuracy with extreme positions that the sun and moon would have occupied in prehistoric times.

It is well known that on the day of the summer solstice an alignment taken from the "altar stone" to the "heel stone" at Stonehenge will pinpoint the position of the sunrise, and every year tourists gather to witness the phenomenon. What is not so well known is that no less than 12 significant extreme positions of the sun, and 12 of the moon, are accurately pinpointed by Stonehenge alignments. The astronomical, geometrical, and engineering ingenuity involved in establishing and preserving these alignments is astonishing enough in itself. It is even more so when it is considered that the Stonehenge complex was developed in three distinct stages over three centuries, and the later engineers and builders managed to place their stones so skillfully that the alignments established in the original structure were never obscured.

According to Professor Hawkins, who was supported by the famous British astonomer Professor Fred Hoyle, Stonehenge was a gigantic and complex astronomical clock with a built-in computer capable of accurately predicting lunar eclipses. This was achieved by the positioning of six stones, three black ones and three white ones, in the 56 holes now known as the Aubrey

Below: for the tourist Stonehenge appears abruptly, an improbable circle of massive stones set in the midst of the calm English farming country. For scientists like Hawkins, Stonehenge is not a peculiar heap of stones but a precise instrument that can be readily and accurately deciphered.

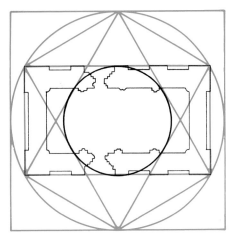

Above: John Michell's scheme of the cosmological foundation of Glastonbury, showing the plan of St. Mary's Chapel, the site of the original circular wattle chapel. The square enclosing the outer circle has dimensions that, according to Michell, show it was a microcosm of the New Jerusalem. The outer circle has an area of 166.5, which by gematria is related to the Spirit of the Earth. Below: St. Mary's Chapel today.

holes and dug by the first builders of Stonehenge. But why should succeeding generations of brilliant mathematicians and engineers over a period of 300 years have bent all their efforts on the task of constructing an astronomical clock? Various tentative suggestions have been put forward. One is that the astronomical clock served the need of a farming community to determine the right time for the planting of crops. Another is that it served to maintain and enhance the power of a dominant priesthood over an ignorant and subdued populace. A third is that it was an intellectual exercise engaged in by men seeking ever more complex mathematical and engineering problems to test their powers.

A still different explanation is given by the best-selling English author John Michell. In *The View over Atlantis* published in 1969, and *City of Revelation* published in 1972, he has developed a theory that the Temple of Jerusalem, the Great Pyramid, Stonehenge, and Glastonbury all incorporate the same principles and proportions in their construction, and that these and other structures throughout the world are evidence of the existence of a worldwide prehistoric civilization. In that civilization according to Michell, religion, magic, astronomy, and a technology that he calls "sonic engineering" belonged together in a grand design that harmoniously united the heavens and the earth, humankind and Nature. Michell reads the riddles of the stones as clues that could lead to the recovery of the lost arts and sciences of the bygone Golden Age he described.

Basing his ideas on numerology and gematria, Michell puts forward the suggestion that both Stonehenge and Glastonbury were structures designed with incredible subtlety on principles accredited to traditional magic for the purpose of collecting, storing, and transmitting solar energy. He quotes the work of a Scottish psychic, Foster Forbes, who visited numerous prehistoric sites to try to describe their history and meaning through his sense of touch. The ability to do this is called psychometry, and its existence is scientifically acknowledged. In 1938 Forbes published the book *The Unchronicled Past*. In it he asserted that stone circles were erected "not only in conjunction with astronomical observation by the advanced priesthood"—a discovery later confirmed by both Thom and Hawkins—"but that the actual sites should serve in some measure as receiving stations for direct influences from heavenly constellations that were known and appreciated by the priesthood—especially at certain seasons of the year." This view immediately brings us back from cautious, rational speculation based on known scientific principles to magic, to the hermetic idea of "as above, so below," to Marsilio Ficino's idea of the *spiritus mundi*, and even to gematria and numerology.

One of the more arcane traditions of number magic is that there is associated with each planet a numerological magic square, which is the key to the control of the planet's influence and power. The magic squares were believed to express mathematically the motions of the planetary orbits, and to contain a formulation of a pattern of natural growth. For example, the magic square of the sun consists of 36 figures and is as follows:

6	32	3	34	35	1
7	11	27	28	8	30
19	14	16	15	23	24
18	20	22	21	17	13
25	29	10	9	26	12
36	5	33	4	2	31

This may look like a random jumble of figures, but a closer study will reveal that if one figure were altered, or if two were made to change places the symmetry of the whole square would collapse. Add together any row, column, or diagonal: the total is always 111. Add together the corner numbers of the square, 6, 1, 36, 31: they total 74. Move inward toward the center and add the corner numbers of the smaller square formed by 11, 8, 29, 26: again the total is 74. Add the total of the four numbers at the very center, 16, 15, 22, 21: it is also 74. Add together the numbers around the perimeter: the total is 370. The total sum of all the 36 numbers in the square is 666.

From this are drawn the potent magical numbers of the sun: 36, 111, 74, 370, and 666. Whole multiples of the magic numbers are taken to be as potent as the numbers themselves. According to Michell's analysis Stonehenge was laid out on a plan that incorporated these numbers, so functioning as a magical instrument for the control of solar power. The perimeter of the circular earthwork surrounding Stonehenge measures 370 MY. A hexagon drawn within this circle has an area of 66,600 square feet or 7400 square yards. The circle formed by the Aubrey holes has an area of 6660 square yards. A line drawn through the center of the inner ring would form the axis of two intersecting circles of 666 feet circumference, or alternatively a side of an equilateral triangle of area 44,400 feet (6 times 7400). The bluestone circle has an area of 666 square MY. Furthermore, if two triangles are placed within the circle of the outer earthwork in the form of Solomon's seal—that is, overlapping to form a six-sided star—each of their sides will measure 3330 inches (half of 6660 and 3 times 1110) or 277.5 feet. This latter number is held to be significant because 2775 is the sum of all the numbers from 1 to 74, and 277.5 is also the radius of a circle with a circumference of 1746. This number, 1746, is "the cabalistic number of fusion," and Stonehenge, according to this theory, was constructed in order to bring about a fusion of solar and terrestrial forces.

Assuming that Michell's measurements are accurate, the mathematic and geometric calculations based on them can be checked and found to be correct. A valid objection might be made that Michell proves his point by skipping from one unit of measurement to another, using the inch, the foot, the yard, and the MY to suit his purpose. But let us suspend skepticism for the time being and follow his argument further.

Glastonbury, according to Michell, was also designed on a pattern dictated by the principal numbers of the magic square of the sun. The authority for this information is none other than the controversial Bligh Bond, cabalist and former architect

Above: the cosmic temple of Stonehenge by John Michell. Again the figure of St. John's New Jerusalem is superimposed over the reconstructed ground plan of Stonehenge. As the Jerusalem square and the outer circle have exactly the same perimeter (316.8 feet), and the inner square exactly contains the bluestone circle, "The New Jerusalem is Stonehenge with the circle squared," Michell writes.

Above: Alfred Watkins was a retired English businessman who had a sudden vision in which the countryside was crossed by a system of lines linking ancient sites. He called them ley lines.

in charge of work on the abbey ruins. Bligh Bond laid out a ground plan of the abbey in the form of a rectangular grid of 36 squares, 36 figures comprising the square of the sun. A side of each of these squares measures 74 feet or 888 inches, and the whole rectangle measures 666 feet by 296 feet (4 times 74). The area of each of the 36 squares is 74 square MY, and the area of the whole rectangle is 26,640 square MY (666 times 40) or, to bring in another of the units of measurements of antiquity, 666,000 square cubits (1 cubit = 1.72 feet).

According to these calculations it appears that Glastonbury was founded on identical principles to those employed by the people who built Stonehenge between 1500 and 2000 years before the first Christian church was erected. The theory is that Glastonbury was conceived not only as a place of Christian worship, but also like Stonehenge to attract solar energy.

There might seem to be a contradiction in the idea that prehistoric man and the early Christian saints applied the same principles of building, but John Michell believes that early Christianity embraced a magical tradition based on numerology and "sacred geometry" which had been handed down from remotest antiquity. Furthermore, the tradition survived into the Middle Ages, and Gothic cathedrals all over Europe were expressly designed on magical principles to attract some specific celestial power. The ancient secrets were preserved by members of the medieval guilds, particularly the masons, and were

Right: the ley lines joining the "camps" of Credenhill, Magna, and Brinsop. These are the spaces enclosed by ancient earth embankments, generally on the top of a hill or on high ground. According to Watkins, every camp had at least one ley line touching its boundary or passing through the highest point. Either leys were planned as tracks to camps, Watkins wrote, or camps were placed by leys already in existence. He believed the leys came first.

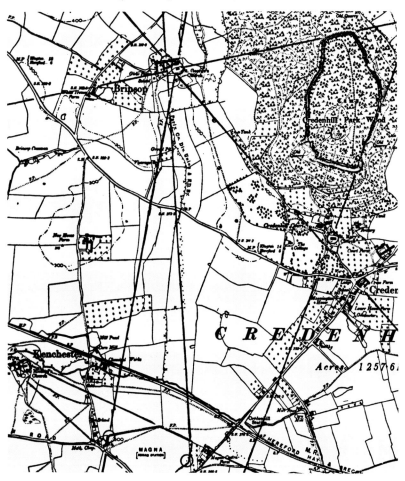

applied without the consent or knowledge of the Church.

For good measure, Michell also demonstrates that the Great Pyramid was constructed according to an identical system and for a similar purpose as Stonehenge, but in relation to the planetary influence of mercury instead of the sun. This is how his theory emerges of an ancient worldwide civilization founded on a science that involved numbers, proportions, and a belief in the possibility and usefulness of focusing celestial forces and influences. The belief was carried out by means of stone structures arranged in certain patterns, and often situated in calculated relation to features in the surrounding landscape.

That isn't the whole story. In fact it is little more than half the story. The rest of it concerns terrestrial forces and influences as well.

In the early 1920s a 65-year-old English merchant and amateur archeologist, Alfred Watkins, was out riding in the hills in his native Herefordshire. He pulled up in order to view the familiar landscape, and suddenly saw it as he had never seen it before, criss-crossed by straight lines that intersected at churches and at points marked by ancient stones. It was a visionary experience and, as often happens with sudden revelations, it determined the course of the rest of his life's work. He was convinced that he had seen in a flash the landscape of ancient Britain, a landscape covered with a vast network of straight tracks, many of them aligned either with the sun or with the path of a star. He called this network the "ley system."

Working on a special ordnance survey map, Watkins confirmed his vision. He found that straight lines extending many miles could be drawn to pass directly through churches, ancient sites, and man-made landmarks. It seems that for some reason not yet understood by us, but possibly for trade, straight roads were planned long before the Romans. However, because many of these tracks pass through difficult countryside with no attempt to skirt lakes, bogs, or mountains, one is tempted to think there is a deeper significance to them than a system of trade routes. The routes are marked by man-made landmarks such as cairns built on mountain slopes or notches cut in ridges, and various ancient sites.

Watkins was ridiculed for his theory because the prevailing version of ancient history at that time was that prehistoric Britons were little more than painted savages. But he stuck to his view and amassed a great deal of evidence which he published in 1925 in *The Old Straight Track*. Gradually other antiquarians became convinced, and began to investigate too.

One of these was Guy Underwood, another amateur archeologist who learned dowsing, or water divining, in order to carry out his investigations. His research with his divining rod took him to old churches and ancient sites of traditional sanctity all over the country. He found that at the center of every circle of stones, and at a key point in every church he examined, there was an underground source of energy. A number of water lines converged in a radiating pattern to this spot. He called the spot a "blind spring." But he also found two other underground lines of force, not necessarily connected with the water line, which responded to the divining rod. One of these lines, which

The Old Straight Tracks

Alfred Watkins was a down-to-earth businessman. He had lived his entire life in Herefordshire, England, as generations of his ancestors had before him. He was more familiar than most with the look of the land around him, for he had spent his working life as a representative for a brewery, traveling from village to village and town to town in his daily work.

One day as he was riding across the hills, he pulled up his horse to look out over the familiar landscape stretched out below him. Suddenly, in a vision like a lightning flash, he saw a network of lines standing out like brightly glowing wires across the surface of the countryside. They met at the sites of churches, ancient stones, and castles.

Watkins embarked upon an intensive study of the line system. He found that ancient sites throughout the countryside could be connected on Ordnance Survey maps by absolutely straight lines. He named them "ley" lines because many ancient places with names ending in -ley, -ly, and -leigh were found along these straight tracks. For the rest of his life he maintained that his first unexpected glimpse of the line network had been complete and accurate. His studies only verified his vision.

he called an "aquastat," seemed in some way to govern the layout of religious monuments and determine the positioning of stones, ditches, or buildings. The other, which he called a "track line," seemed to govern the route of roads and tracks. Underwood called all these subterranean lines of force "geodetic" lines. He believed that the main use early man had made of them was to mark out and divide the surface of the Earth. His research led him to the conclusion that both prehistoric and medieval builders had placed sacred sites and aligned the buildings they erected on them in observance of geodetic laws. In other words, they knew of the existence of lines of force running through the earth and, in some way, they had attempted to harness them for beneficial ends. Incidentally, Underwood found that Watkins' surface leys were often paralleled beneath the surface of the earth by a line of force.

In his book *The Pattern of the Past*, published in 1969, Underwood writes ". . . the three geodetic lines, the water line, the aquastat, and the track line appear to have much in common: they appear to be generated within the Earth; to involve wave motion; to have great penetrative power; to form a network on the face of the Earth; to affect the germination and manner of growth of certain trees and plants; to be perceived and used by animals; to affect opposite sides of the animal body, and to form spiral patterns." From these observations he goes on to say that they seem to be controlled by mathematical laws that involve the number 3 in their construction and the number 7 in their spiral patterns. These two numbers have been accorded arcane meaning from the earliest times. Underwood sees these geodetic lines as manifestations of an Earth Force, an idea which was central to many ancient religions. Traces of this belief can still be found throughout the world today.

When the bustling, expansionist, industrialized civilization of Western Europe tried to carry its influence into China about a century ago, its pioneers suffered a great deal of frustration and exasperation. For example, a proposal to cut a railway tunnel through a hill would be met by a polite refusal from the Chinese authorities. Their explanation would be that that particular range of hills was a terrestrial dragon, and that to cut through its tail was forbidden. Proposed sites for factories were firmly rejected for reasons that seemed to Europeans equally superstitious and nonsensical. They had not understood that in China there was an ancient and important belief in lines of force, known as "dragon current," running all over the surface of the Earth. Before any building was erected, or any tree planted, an expert known as a geomancer had to be consulted as to how the current would be affected. The Chinese were amazed on their side that the technologically advanced Europeans had no conception of this venerable science.

As everything else in Chinese philosophy, the dragon current was divided into yin and yang. The yin, or female current, was supposed to flow along gentle undulating countryside, and the yang, or male force, through steep high peaks. The most favorable position was felt to be where the two currents of yin and yang met. This was therefore often selected by a geomancer as a site for a tomb because the Chinese believed that the influences

Above: the Long Man of Wilmington, a figure that appears in the chalky white ground when the turf is cut away. It is in Sussex, England where the ground, called "downs," is of chalk composition. Watkins believed that the staves held by the Long Man were for surveying. It is thought that this figure dates from pre-Roman times.

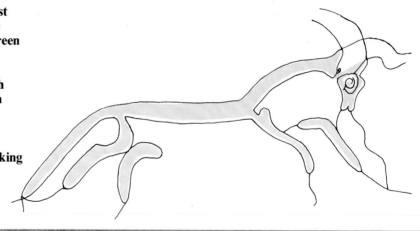

surrounding their dead ancestors played a decisive role in the future of their family.

Geomancers interpreted the earth in terms of the sky, rather like the principle of "as above, so below" that recurs so many times in ancient philosophy and magic. Mountains were thought of as stars, and large rivers as the Milky Way. Each main dragon current had small tributaries or veins, and every small vein had its own astrological interpretation. Different parts of the Earth were thought to come under the influence of the different planets then known—Jupiter, Mars, Venus, Mercury, and Saturn. These planets in turn had correspondences with colors, materials, landscape characteristics, animals, parts of the body, and so on. Between the planets and the various correspondences was a complex system of harmony and discord. As John Michell writes in *The View over Atlantis:* ". . . Venus can go with Saturn but not with Mars. Thus a high rounded hill will harmonize with one with a flat top but not with a sharp mountain peak. The two could not therefore stand together. Where nature had

Above: the White Horse as it appears from the air today. It is 350 feet long, and on clear days is visible for 15-20 miles. There is an old superstition that a wish will come true if someone stands on the Horse's eye and turns around three times.

139

placed two hills in discord, Chinese geomancers had the shape of one altered. The top of the peak would be cut off or the rounded hill sharpened with an earthwork or flattened into a high plateau. In this way the paths of the various influences across the country were visibly defined, the very bones of the landscape altered to reflect the celestial symmetry."

On the Nazca plains of Peru a remarkable network of straight lines, together with various figures of men, animals, and symbols, has been etched. The paths and figures were created by removing stones and pebbles to expose the dark earth beneath. It was first discovered by pilots flying over the region. One of the many interpretations is that they are sun paths, so arranged that a person moving along a certain path at the solstice or equinox would see the sun rising or setting on the horizon, straight ahead.

In the course of her travels in Tibet, Alexandra David-Neel saw several "lung-gom-pas runners." These men travel for days across the country without stopping, maintaining an extraordinary speed and proceeding by leaps so that they seem to rebound from the earth each time their feet touch it. They always pursue exactly straight tracks, even when these lead over mountains. Alexandra David-Neel supposed that the runners' strength must be the result of prolonged physical and spiritual training. No doubt this was a part of it, but the fact that they pursued straight tracks even when these led over difficult terrain suggests, in the light of what we now know, that they might have possessed the secret of harnessing the earth force. Really advanced lung-gom-pas, it is said, could glide through the air without ever touching the ground with their feet.

In other words they could fly. There are many legends of feats of magical flight performed by the ancient Britons. Bladud, an ancient magician said to fly using stones, crashed where St. Paul's Cathedral now stands in London. But another British magician, Abiris, is said to have flown all the way to Greece without mishap. Fairy tales? Perhaps. But John Michell has a theory about magical flight. He believes that flying on a stone or other conveyance was made possible by using the magnetic force of the leys, which harnessed celestial energy. Many of the mysterious buildings of antiquity, he believes—notably Stonehenge and the Pyramids—were constructed in order to effect this fusion of terrestrial and celestial forces. This is why the cabalistic number for fusion, 1746, is to be found in their proportions. Furthermore, the energies thus generated could be employed for numerous other purposes, especially the construction of the huge monuments that survive today.

Some would say that to speculate so wildly is irresponsible. But the mysteries remain. There is no doubt that the impressive achievements of our technological civilization have been bought at a price and have resulted in a loss of coordination between human beings and their environment. Both are in jeopardy today. Perhaps we should no longer dismiss the magical and psychic sciences of our remote forebears as nonsense and superstition. In the present plight of the world, perhaps we could do with a little magic—which might just be another name for a long-lost science.

Right: a long perfectly straight ley line cuts sharply through the English countryside. Could it possibly be purely chance, or is there a message waiting there from some dimly perceived figure in the past, just waiting for the clues to be properly read?

The Occult Sciences and Modern Man

What do magic and the occult sciences have to offer modern man? Are they ways of coming to terms with reality, or of escaping from it? These are questions we all have to find our own answers to. Some would say that occult pursuits have nothing to offer; that to dabble in them is to repudiate reason and true science; that a belief in magic and the supernatural is to regress to the age of supersition or to a childish mentality which uncritically accepts all marvels just because they are marvelous.

There may be an element of truth in this reasoning. The wave of occultism sweeping the Western world today undoubtedly owes some of its appeal to its elements of sensationalism, irrationality, sexuality, and violence. But to maintain that these are the sole reasons for its appeal is to adopt a rigid one-sided view, and to ignore the many positive aspects.

That the planets can significantly influence our lives; that our character and destiny is encoded in our name number; that verbal spells can be effective for good or evil; that demons or the spirits of the dead can be summoned up by means of ritual: these are all statements about the objective world and the laws that govern it. In theory they should be able to be conclusively proved or disproved, and until they are we are at liberty to choose to believe or disbelieve them. But even if they were conclusively disproved as objective facts about the world and its laws, this would not make them unworthy of consideration. It cannot be denied that such beliefs have been a part of the furniture of the human mind for thousands of years, and still are today. The beliefs may be partially or totally wrong, but the fact that they have survived for so long is significant. Such beliefs should not necessarily be taken as an indication of stupidity and superstition. They may just as well signify the human aspiration to find order in, and to make sense of, our total environment. It may also signify the mind's longing for a broader grasp of things, for an expanded reality.

Reality is limited for all of us. For some it is limited to the kitchen, the supermarket, the nursery, and the television; others may take in the office and the highway. We may read books, go to church, the theater or opera, travel in foreign countries in order to take in a bit more of reality. But however full a life we may live, we all know at bottom that there is much more in life and the world than we can ever hope to experience or to know. We can, however, experience and know more than we do at present. To accomplish this expansion we need to do two things. We need first to understand the nature of our limitations and distinguish between those that are fixed and immutable (our sense of smell and hearing will never compete for sharpness with a dog's, for instance) and those that can be laid to laziness, lack of curiosity, or unquestioning acceptance of prevailing ideas. Secondly, we need to expose ourselves to the influence of other realities, other cultures and world views, other ways of life.

Magic and the occult or psychic sciences are important because they are based on a different concept of reality than the one that has shaped our normal world. It is at least worth considering that what they appeal to in us is not just primitive lust for power and sensation, but a need—which is perhaps also primitive—for a unified science and philosophy.

Impressive though the achievements of Western technological science are, there is no denying that they have been bought at a price, which includes increased nervous strain and destruction of the Earth's natural riches. In the interests of progress, productivity, and the accumulation of personal or corporate wealth, we have exploited our fellow human beings, nature, and the environment for centuries. We are only just waking up to the fact that the exploited can kick back in unexpected ways. Our reaction to the kick-back tends to escalate the problem because we always think in terms of more of the same. Our answer to the evils of technology is more and better technology. If rivers are becoming polluted, the solution is, we reason today, to develop stronger, and therefore costlier, antipollutants.

Perhaps we should not dismiss the magical and psychical sciences of our forebears as readily as we do. A return to the magical view of the world might be the start of a solution. Why? Because fundamental to the old beliefs is the idea that the world is a grand design, a totality in which the parts are all interrelated, interresponsive, and interdependent, so that whatever happens to the part affects the whole and vice versa. Many of the ills of the modern world can be traced to a neglect of this fundamental principle.

To measure the positions of old stones, to probe the secrets of number and words, to explore inner space with the aid of cabalistic symbolism or ritual, is surely less irresponsible than the activities of many technocrats dedicated to the pursuit of progress, productivity, and affluence. There may be no magical solution to the world's problems, but the unified philosophy that the magical view of the world is based on is more likely ultimately to yield a satisfactory long-term solution than an approach that looks for a solution in terms of "more of the same."

Picture Credits

Key to picture positions: (T) top (C) center (B) bottom; and in combinations, e.g. (TR) top right (BL) bottom left